T0147375

# Dedications/ In Between The Two

Tia McDaniel

iUniverse, Inc.
New York Bloomington

**Dedications/In Between The Two**



*iUniverse books may be ordered through booksellers or by contacting:*

*iUniverse*
*1663 Liberty Drive*
*Bloomington, IN 47403*
*www.iuniverse.com*
*1-800-Authors (1-800-288-4677)*



*ISBN: 978-1-4401-3799-0 (pbk)*
*ISBN: 978-1-4401-3800-3 (ebk)*

*Printed in the United States of America*

*iUniverse rev. date: 4/15/2009*

# ACKNOWLEDGMENTS

I couldn't have done this without the man up above I thank him for putting me through obstacles. Even when I wanted to give up he gave me another reason to keep going and look at me I'm finally making one of my dreams come to reality. I'm excited and anxious to see the response whether it's negative or positive some way and some how it'll help me become even a better author. I would like to thank the people that inspired me to write my book the stories that you have shared with me made me realize I'm not the only one. I would also like to thank my step-dad James Megginson for helping me out. My daddy Tony McDaniel my mother Rosella Megginson my sister Tierra McDaniel. My loved ones especially my cousin Miketa Turner. Ashley Knowlenberg, Brandon Smith, Ashley Sandidge, Raven Booth, Conita Sandidge, Roy Thompson, Ladie Morris, Charity Morris, Jasmine Morris, Khristine Thomas, Alicia Blakey, Kiyona Ware, Trevor Booker, Thomas Smith, Poem McIntosh Aleeyah Brown, Dominique Haynes, Kim Gibson and Tiffany Tinsley. To Mark Rodriguez thank you for working as the graphic designer loved your ideas. To my models for the book thanks for showing off them sexy looks of yours (LOL). If there is anyone I missed you are not forgotten. And to my readers thank you for even picking up my book and looking into my work. I love you all and I truly thank you and to people who told me that I couldn't do it I just have four words for you. LOOK AT ME NOW! And thank you Iuniverse!!!!!!!!!!

Love
Tia McDaniel

# DEDICATIONS

Monica who is known as mama she was given that name from her loved ones because she was known to correct, provide, and support anyone in need. Along with her friends Monique, Neka, Lasha, and Serena. Monique who is known as the ghetto misses, Neka as the black Barbie doll, Lasha as the Spanish princess, and Serena as the white chocolate which bundled together as the junior mint. Monique, Neka, and Serena were all mothers. They all came from the same neighborhood where most kids wouldn't make it to the age of thirteen. So to keep theirselves off the street they developed their own group called shawties with attitudes. They were an undefeated step team that brought heat to every place they stepped in. Life was a struggle but they tried not to keep that in between their friendship, but tragedy strike everywhere they turned. Monica who was well known for her writing skills was offered a chance to win a scholarship and a book deal but she didn't know what to write about. As time went by things began to happen which touched her heart. She took out her pad and began to write about her life and her friend's life. She wanted to bring forth what other's were to afraid to talk about and by doing this she had opened up eyes of the people that looked down on them and later made a change.

# Chapter 1

## The Contest

`Monica stops at the letter t that was suppose to finish the word 'statement' looking up over towards the clock she watched the black thick handle slowly move up closer to the nine. In a rush to get out of class she mumbles amongst herself "Come on bell ring" biting her lower lip and tapping her foot heavily on the floor. Ms. Jones looks up from her studies taking off her glasses that were pushed up against her face as if she was blind as a bat. "Did you say something Monica?" Ms. Jones asked curiously. Monica looks over at Ms. Jones; shaking her head "No!" Monica said. "I didn't say anything." As soon as Monica began to speak again the bell rings, waking up the kids that were sleeping and interrupting conversations that were going on that had nothing to do with the work that was assigned to them. Students rushed out of the classrooms into the hallway carrying on with their gossip that they had intended on finishing.

As Monica stood to pick up her books she noticed Ms. Jones staring at her from across the room. "Monica could you come here for a second?" Ms. Jones asked. Monica raises her eyebrow as she starts walking over to Ms. Jones's desk wondering what she had done now. "Yes?" Monica stood at Ms. Jones "Monica your story was very good." Monica went into a daze while watching Ms. Jones move her hands around. "Have you thought about entering into the short story contest that the school is sponsoring?" Ms. Jones asked. "No, I haven't I've been too busy with other things." Monica replied. Ms. Jones was shocked to hear this excuse of Monica's. "Well if you do decide to do it please don't hesitate to come see me. There is a twenty thousand dollar scholarship for the winner, and you have the talents for this." Ms. Jones exclaimed looking at Monica hoping that she would think about the offer. "Okay I will think on that." Monica replied back hoping that she would end the conversation at that.

Monique peaks through the crack of the door. "Monica would you come on" she rudely interrupts. Monica looks over towards Monique and whispers "Would you shut up?" Monique throws her head up in the air and back down "O no she did not!" Monica turns back to Ms. Jones and smiles. "Thank you; if I do decide to enter I will let you know." She said. "All right thank you for your time." Ms. Jones replied. Monique began speaking in an impatient matter. Frustrated with the hold up she speaks again. "Monica would you hurry up you know I gotta get this kitchen done" running her fingers through her hair.

Monica walks toward the door but an interruption stopped her in her tracks. "Monique, baby you need a perm. Girl you know you gotta get them monthly." Ms. Jones announced in a humor manner. Monique tempts to pull off a smile. "Thanks for letting me know" then she frowns "Even though I already knew that." Monique said. "No problem girl." Ms. Jones replied back while throwing up her hand. Monica walks out the door closing it behind her. The two of them began walking towards the car Monique pops her gum. "She is always geeking up on me. What she should do is get rid of that monster boyfriend of hers' looking like Freddy Kruger. And besides what was ya'll talking about? She asks. Monica looks over to Monique "My essay; she told me I should enter into the short story contest." She said. "Girl you should your stories are good and if you win you need to split that scholarship fifty-fifty. I would enter into that contest too if I was as good of a writer as you, but I'm into the fashion world." Monique said. "What?" cocking her eyebrow. "Girl please only them rich know it all folks win contests like that." Monica explained. "Honey don't be letting anybody get in your way when it comes to your dreams and goals. You to good for that." Monique said. "You know I be having them dejavus. I see you walking with your head high Gucci heels on switching those typhoon hips of yours and letting them know you there to take over." Monique replied taking in a deep breath and snapping her fingers.

"Girl I ran out of breath on that speech." Monique said. "Mmm hmm!" Monica replied.. "Why you say that? It's hard for teens like us from the ghetto to get scholarships especially the harsh society we living in. It's a recession going out in the world and ain't nothing coming to us in a silver platter." Monique walks in front of Monica and stops her "Monica you are the next big thing to let the world know there is room for a sister or brother from the ghetto to get the same education a rich person can get." Monique announced.

Monica and Monique put their books in the back of the seat and gets into the car. Monica looks over to Monique, "We'll see" Monica replies back.

"Anyways where was Neka today?" Monique questioned fed up with the conversation, "Umm, she had to go and get her checkup." Monica said. "Her baby is going to look exactly like C.J." Monica said. Monique looks at Monica "As sexy as he is I guess so." "Girl you and your mouth when will you ever stop and think about what you are going to say?" Monica said. "I don't feel like it, it takes up too much time. How many times do I have to explain this to people?" Monique said. Laughing amongst herself.

Monica pulls up to Neka's house reaching in the back seat she grabs her journal beginning to write. "Girl you always writing in that journal. What do you be writing about?" Monique question. "I just take notes you know what goes on everyday it's like a therapy session all in one small black book." She said. "Well what do you write in that book?" Monique questioned again. Monica smiles "I can't tell." She said. "Mhm" reaching over Monica, Monique beeps the horn continually. "Move them titties of yours". She said. Serena walks out of the house hollering, "why you keep beeping that horn we coming." Monique pokes her head out of the window. "I told ya'll I had to get my hair done." Monique hollered out. Serena, Lasha, and Neka walked out of the house to the car. Serena opens the door for Neka, as Neka crept into the car Monique announces, "My goodness you look like a grapefruit!" "A watermelon." "A beach ball." "A" before Monique could finish Neka interrupts her. "Well thank you Mo you sure do know how to put a girl down." Neka said. Monique smiles and throws up her hand "O you welcome."

"I can't wait until I have him. My back is starting to hurt real badly and my feet are swollen." Neka said. "Well you know what that mean, don't you?" Monica asked. "Na, what do it mean?" Neka asked while rubbing her stomach. "It means you might have an early pregnancy." She said. "O, I hope so this baby is one heavy ass load." "I'm tired of the constant peeing and the pain. The sooner the better." Neka replied.

Monica pulls up to the salon Monique pokes her head out the window looking over to the next parking space and spots Trey'shaun. "There goes my man right there looking fine and fly as ever. Monique walks over to Trey' Shaun's car peaks through the car window banging and questions "Where Nya at? "She at the house helping my ma make dinner for tonight." Trey' Shaun replied. "Did you take her to get her ears done like I asked you to? She questions again. "Yea baby, don't sweat it." Trey' Shaun said. He grabs Monique's butt and pulls her closer to him and kisses her. She looks up at him and smiles licking her lips. "Baby you trying to show off?" Monique speaks aloud. "If I got a shawty like you who is the mother of my child, who loves me unconditionally, and got ass and thighs like that, hell yeah! I'ma show off." Trey' Shaun announces. Monique smiles even harder. Boy stop! She laughs. "So baby what you about to get done." He asked. "Im going to get my hair, and nails done." Monique replied. "O, you need any extra money?" Trey' Shaun asked. "No thank you baby im straight for right now." But Monique was hungry for money. "I'ma take a hundred for later." "Ok baby girl." He looks over to the car.

"Wait; is that Monica over there?" "Yea that's her." Trey' Shaun calls Monica over. "Aye Monica, come here for a second." Monica starts walking towards them "What do you want Trey?" Monica said. "I just wanted to know if you going to my party tonight you know my homeboy Damon is going to be there." Trey' Shaun said. "And? I care because?" she said. "M why you tripping he is not a bad person." Monique questions. "Your boy needs to get a hold of himself and im not talking bout grabbing his dick and shit. Im talking bout all them nasty ass skeet's he be having around him." Monica said. "Man, Damon doesn't want them girls he got better sense then that. Ya dig what im saying?" Trey' Shaun said. "I'll think about it Trey." She says. Monique interrupts while rubbing his chest "Baby we going to get at you later." She starts to suckle on Trey' Shaun's lip he grabs her butt again. "Damn this never gets old to me." Trey' Shaun said. "Eww, I am still here." Monica said in disgust, Trey' Shaun waves Monica on to leave. Her head rows back "O, no the hell he didn't" she says aloud and walks away.

"Thank you Debbie! You got a shawty looking good all over again." Monique said while messing with her hair. "You welcome baby." Debbie replied. "Now we can go to this throw down tonight ya'll, and show these other squads how we do this." Monica said. "Yea! There is no other step team out there that can beat us we are undefeated and we going to remain undefeated ya dig." Lasha announced. "Word boo, we going to kill em. First we are going to diss their crew with our viscous flow then we going to step on their faces with our ridiculous J's then the finishing touches we going to kill them with our deadly swag. Can I get a amen." Serena exclaimed. "AMEN!" they said aloud throwing up their hands. "Where is this throw down going to be at?" Debbie asked chewing on her monkey bread. "It's going to be at Strawberries that new club down Main Street. Everybody is going to be there." Lasha said. "Yep, we got these new outfits that we purchased just for this night." Serena said. "O okay ima make sure I make a appearance tonight then." Debbie said. The girls hug Debbie and walks out of the building.

"Can I get a beat DJ? I would like to welcome ya'll to the two thousand and eight step team throw down. Where the best step teams come out to perform to win five thousand five hundred dollars in cash." The announcer said. "Please give a round of applause to the teams Sassy Ladies, Thin ice, and SWA." The audience started to cheer on their favorite step team. Monica and the crew marched onto the floor to give their first performance. Monica announces "Attention! SWA is here to please you with a step that you'll never forget leaving sad faces against our opponents, and leave the crowd roaring with excitement now please don't leak on our floors with the adrenaline rush in your body we know we sexy. SWA what do we stand for?" Monica asked. "Maam we stand for shawties with attitudes." Serena said. "Feisty, and fierce at the same time we rock our hater blockers!" Lasha said. "And we come to step and make a beat all over ya'lls face owwww!" Monique said. As the crew started stepping the crowd was going wild.

After every team performed it was a tie. "Man I can't believe this. A tie? They must be out their minds we never tie up with another team. And my baby kicking the hell out of me." Neka said. "Alright chica's we got to go into the battle round Neka you going to need to sit down on this one you to pregnant to continue." Monica said. The two final teams performed one last round. "Ladies and Gents you have just seen two teams perform, so who do you think should take home in this money tonight?" the announcer said. As he waved his hand over the teams the crowd screamed louder for SWA. Lasha, Monica, Monique, Serena, and Neka look at each other with excitement one last performance together. "Yea baby yea!" Neka said aloud. "Bravo ladies!" clapping his hands. "Ya'll were off the chain tonight. And Neka you was working that floor girlfriend with your cute little pregnant figure." Jerome said while fiddling with his braids. Neka laughs and hugs Jerome. "Who you here with?" Neka asks. "O boo look over to your left you see that fine piece of foreign I got over there." Jerome said. "Yea I see him he a cutie." Neka said. "I know baby girl and I noticed that thick don't only come in black packages if." Looking down "if you know what I mean." He said while snapping his fingers. "And baby if I'm wrong then there is no right." Jerome said. "I'll catch up with ya'll later I got some business to handle." He said. "Okay do what you do baby!" Monique announced. "You know it!" Jerome hollers out twiddling his fingers in the air.

Congratulations girls you all were something else on that floor. I'm not just saying that because I know ya'll. That dance you did in the middle of the step was real good. I might need you to teach me that." Debbie said laughing amongst herself. "We got you Ms. Debbie cakes." Monique said. Monica laughs and then snorts. "My bad." Monica said.

# Chapter 2

## Pain and Connection

Monica straightens up her dresser when she hears the phone ring. Hello? Hey, Mena! "How are you Monique?" She asks. "I'm good; can't complain." Monique replies back. "And how is the family?" Mena questions. "They doing fine. Nya getting into mostly everything her hands can get on." She said. "That's good and that's what kids do, but did you want to speak to Monica?" "Yeah" Monique announced.

Mena calls out for Monica. "Monica telephone", Tierra bends over the couch looking into the hallway and hollers out "Monica you bet not hold up that phone I gots me a brother to talk to." Tierra said. "What you need to do is take your little ass to sleep with your frisky self." Mena replies.

"Who is it?" Monica questions. "Its Monique get the phone!" Monica picks up the phone in her room. "Hey girl!" Monica said. "Hey, are you coming to the party." Monique asked. "No, I'm not!" Monica hollered out into the phone. "Why not? You need to meet Damon. Im telling you he knows how to treat a girl right. That's my buddy. He not like them other brothers out here." Monica pauses and sighs, "All right I'm only going so you can stop bugging me but no Damon." Monica replied back. "Okay girl I'ma be at your house in about thirty-five minutes." "What?" Monica questioned. " M I knew you would go."

"Ugh I swear you a trip. I love you too girl make sure you be ready. Okay see you when you get here.

Monica hung up the phone trying to race against time she rushes into the bathroom almost falling from the slippery floor that was covered with water. Ma! She hollers out from the bathroom. "What?" Mena hollered back. "Who was the last person up in the bathroom?" she asked in frustration. "Why?" Mena questioned. "I almost fell due to water on the floor!" Monica yelled. "You shouldn't have been running and Tierra!" Mena hollered out from the living room. "Yes." Tierra said in innocence knowing that she was guilty for the massive spill in the bathroom. "What did I tell you about taking a bath and then splashing water everywhere in the bathroom and not cleaning up behind yourself?" Mena questions. Commanding Tierra to come next to where she was sitting Tierra slowly crept towards Mena with her hands on her tail. Mena quickly grabs a hold of Tierra's shirt. "Don't play with me. Ya hear?" Mena asked. "Yes maam. I promised not to do it again." Tierra announced even though she was just trying not to get a whooping she jumps on her mother's lap and kisses her. "Mommy I love you and I thank you for getting after me for doing bad." Tierra said. Mena smiles at Tierra "Now you know I'm not going to fall for that Tierra go on ahead and finish doing what you gotta do." Mena announced. "Ma!" Monica hollered out from the shower. "What you want now?" Mena asked. "I am going with Monique tonight to Trey'Shauns party." "All right you be careful and be home by eleven you know you got to work tomorrow. And I'm not calling in nowhere to tell them your sick when you at home sleeping." There was a sudden knock at the door Mena walks over towards the door as she opens it she finds to see Monique smiling hard. "Who is that at the door ma?" Monica asked. "It's Monique." Mena replied back. I'm coming! Hold up! Monica rushes to her room with water dripping from her hair. Quickly picking out a red shirt she dabs her skin with the towel that lay on the bed. Monica picks up her black beaded necklace that hung from her dresser with the rest of her jewelry then she slides on a pair of her skinny dark blue jeans that she hadn't worn since she had gotten them. She runs out of the room back to the bathroom. Putting her hair into a low side ponytail her baby hair laid on her sides. She then puts on her gold hoop earrings to give even more spark to compliment her eye color, she runs back up the hallway. "Alright I'm ready to go" slapping her thighs. "Umm, are you sure you ready to go I know Adam and Eve walked barefooted but ugh there are shoes made for us now. Monique laughs aloud. Monica looks down at her feet.

"O shoot" Monica said. She walks back to her room and puts on her black and red Nikes. "All right now I'm ready to go." Are you sure this time M?" her mother questioned. Im sure. Monica replies "Aha! You both got jokes." "It is not our fault that you forgot your shoes." Mena replies back.

Arriving at Trey' Shaun's house an hour late. Monique and Monica walks in towards the crowd to meet Trey' Shaun and Damon. Trey' Shaun turns and introduces Damon to Monica. "Damon this is Monica, you remember her from school right?" Trey' Shaun asked. Damon replies back. "Her face look familiar yea I'm pretty sure I know her." Damon says. He reaches for her hand and questions "What's good with you baby girl?" The name is Monica and I ain't your baby girl. Damon holds up his hands "Slow down ma. I didn't mean it like that." Monica crosses her arms "yea ok." Monica stop it and have fun. Monique interrupts.

Yea stop it and have fun. Damon smiling revealing his deep dimples. "I ain't down for that kiddy shit boo so you can quit while you are ahead." Monica replies. "Damn you a mean ass shawty but you just saying this cause you know you can't dance worth nothing." He exclaims. "Excuse me but I can dance I don't know where you been getting your resources from but its telling you wrong." Monica exclaims.

"Well why don't you prove it to me on the floor." Damon said. "Mo hold my prada while I show this boy how I do it." Monica said. Monique grabs a hold of Monica's belongings. Show him what you working with girl. Following Monica to the middle of the dance floor he watches her ass move as she walked. As the two start dancing Monica faces forward with her back towards Damon getting closer to him as the light shines on his forehead showing the glimmers of his sweat. Monica wraps her arms around his neck while he grinds on her. Lasha and Serena walk over towards Monique, and Serena speaks aloud "Dang Monica got a handful of sexiness over at that dance floor." Tarnisha walks pass the crew and rolls her eyes. "I see hoes do get a break from the corner." Monique points her finger in Tarnisha's face "Look here you ugly hefa, I'm not the bitch that opens up my legs to any brother that want pussy." Monique replies back. "Who the fuck is you calling a bitch? Honey I'll give you a bitch. I'm not the one with a child so rewind that shit. You the fucking bitch that opens up their legs from any fool that want cutty because from what I remember your man had some of this too and ate it like it was his last supper. Obviously me and you on the same level shawty. He would of never came to you if I didn't dump him." Tarnisha speaks out in anger. Monique jumps in Tarnisha's face "I will split your weave in two if you don't keep your damn mouth shut. Dirty ass skeet you not even worth my time in jail. Me and Trey' Shaun were friends when he was with you and from what I remember he told me yo pussy smelt like it hadn't been washed in weeks and that it was worn out and stretched out like a fully loaded limo that's been through more checkups then ever so be gone." Tarnisha looks Monique up and down props up her hand "Whatever" and walks away. "That girl ain't got anything better else to do except start drama that's what she is good at and wondering why people talk about her ass." Lasha said. "I know that's right I ain't never seen a girl who is so inconsiderate in my life." Serena exclaimed. "That trick need to get her priorities straight before I straighten it out for her." Monique announced.

Monique Lasha and Serena put their attention back on Monica and Damon and Lasha hollers out. "I see you over there doing your thing I ain't mad at ya." Once Monica hears Lasha she know that she went to far then what she had expected to do. She turns around meeting face to face with Damon. Damon interrupts her thought. "So can I give you a call later on?" Damon asks. She stares at him and gives no reply back. She snaps back into reality when she hears Damon speak again. Yea! Damon pulls out his brand new blackberry storm. He was known to have the new stuff that just hit stores he wasted no time in getting it three four seven sixty- seven eighty- two. Ight shawty I'ma call you. Okay she says in a low toned voice.

Hey Monica we gotta go I got to get some sleep for tomorrow.

Later that night Monica receives a call from Damon. Tierra picks up the phone and answers it. "Hello?" Tierra said. "Hey is Monica there?" Damon said. "Yes she is who are you?" She questions. "Damon!" He replies back Okay hold on let me go get her. Tierra hollers down the hallway "Monica, a boy with a sexy voice named Damon is on the phone. "Okay I got it.," she says. Hello? Monica hears a munching on the phone. I got it Monica hollers out. I'm not on the phone Tierra replies back. Monica hears munching again. Tierra? She hollers out I can hear you. Okay, okay. As Tierra slowly puts down the phone she picks it back up again and announces. "Damon call for me sometime." She finally hangs up the phone. "Hey, Damon." "What's good lil mama?" He asks. "Nothing just laying down and relaxing." Damon questions. "Did you have a good time with me?" "Yeah you were okay but I skilled you on the floor." "Yeah, yeah, you had a little something." "A little something?" Monica questions. "Yes, a little something." Damon said. "Dude you must be out your mind, I had you sweating up a storm." "That's what you think, it was just hot with everybody up on the floor." The conversation continued when Damon asks. "You want to go out tomorrow?" Monica pauses for a second. "Yea! All right I'ma pick you up at nine-tomorrow night." Continuing with their conversation the rest of the night.

Next morning Monica headed off to work when she receives a call from Lasha "Monica! Come to the hospital Neka is expected to go into labor in any time now." Okay I'ma be there in about five minutes." Monica turns and makes a u-turn. As she enters into the hospital she runs up to the main desk and asks the location Neka was at. "Room twenty-eight, second floor." "Thank you" Monica runs to the elevator as she reaches her destination she opens up the door. She looks over towards the bed where Neka lays. Hey girl Neka speaks out while in crucial pain. "Hi NeNe!" Monica replies back. Then Neka starts screaming the doctor and nurses come in to prep Neka up for labor. On the count of three I want you to start pushing. The doctor instructs. As the doctor reaches three Neka starts to push breathing and sweating excessively. "Baby give me your hand." Neka speaks. She grips onto CJ's hand squeezing it even harder CJ try's to show no pain. He calmly says, "Come on baby." A little over twenty minutes Neka gives birth to her baby girl. She hears her baby crying. "Happy birthday to your newborn baby girl. CJ and Neka both smile. As soon as Neka lets go of CJ's hand he starts to rub it from the lack of circulation. She quickly grabs a hold of it again and begins to scream the doctor looks over to Neka and rushes back "Nurse Jay'Merson please come assist me she is having another baby. The doctor pulls out a healthy baby boy. CJ stares while in shock and turns to Neka and says "two" and smiles then passes out. Neka hollers out "CJ wake up, wake up CJ." Monica pulls C.J up on the seat. "Lord have mercy, this boy then passed out." Neka lies back from the tiredness of delivery. Lasha looks over to the babies and smiles “They are so adorable NeNe.” She said. “Thank you.” Neka replied.

# Chapter 3

## Hooters

"Ms.B, you ready?" Monica asks. "Yeah honey I need to get this mess done." Ms. B replied. Ms.B sits down at the sink as Monica cuts on the water to check the temperature. As she runs the water through Ms.B's hair Ms.B announces. "Girl let me tell you, last night I was on a date with my boo." "Your boo?" Monica asks. "Yeah girl my boo." "Ms. B I didn't know you had a boo. Yea honey I woman like me need some muscles around the house. I ain't getting any younger." Ms.B exclaimed. "But anyways he surprised me the other night." "O yea?" Monica said.

Everyone in the salon gave full attention to Ms's. B story. "Anyways last night he took me out to this fancy restaurant trying to be all sentimental." "While I was eating them good ol ribs with barbeque sauce all around my lips he going to get down on his knees and ask me to marry him. Monica? I was so happy that I almost pissed in my pants child I think some of that rib fell out my mouth." Ms.B exclaimed. Everyone in the shop started to laugh. Monica was finally finished with Ms.B's hair as a tall caramel skin male about five- eleven with dark brown wavy hair that could even make fish sea sick around his early thirties come walking into the salon.

The workers and customers start to stare hard. "Hey boo" Ms.B announced. "Hey baby, you ready?" Lamont asked yeah hold on. Monica how much I owe you? Ms. B asks. Thirty-five Monica replied. She hands Monica thirty-five and an extra fifteen. "Thank you Ms.B"

Monica said gracefully. As Ms.B and her man walks out of the salon she looks back at everyone and, winks while pointing at her mans butt. "Work it Ms.B" a customer yells out. Monica laughs while shaking her head.

As Monica is driving home her phone rings. Hello? She said. "What's good baby girl?" Damon asks. "Nothing much heading back home." Monica exclaimed. "So we still on for tonight" Damon ask. She answers with a yes. "Ight, there want be no need for you to dress up this is not going to be no big occasion" Damon replies. "Who said I was going to dress up?" Monica asks.

That night Damon pulls up to Monica's apartment and beeps the horn. Tierra peaks through the window. "Mama there is a ugly black car outside!" Tierra shouts aloud. Damon beeps the horn again. "It's my date." Monica hollers out from her room. Damon beeps the horn again. "If he doesn't stop beeping that horn I'm going out there." Tierra said. Damon beeps the horn again. Tierra walks outside in her pink pajamas over towards Damon. As soon as Tierra starts to speak Damon rolls down the window and she quickly changes her attitude. "Hey cutie! My sister will be down in a minute," Tierra says.

She points to herself "Umm I'ma need you to get out of the car for me I need to check you out. The boys need my permission to take her out." Damon gets out of the car as she swirls her finger around instructing him to turn around. "Turn around, don't be shy now." As he turns around she looks with a surprise and speaks. "Nice butt." Damon asks, "How old are you shorty?" "I'm not short, and I'm old enough to be your mama and tall enough to whoop your ass." "What now youngster?" Tierra said. Damon smiles "You feisty just like your sister" with one hand on her hip and the other pointing at Damon. "Excuse me but do not compare me to her!" Monica walks down the steps.

"Girl get your butt in the house with no jacket on." Monica says. Tierra turns around and starts to switch as she gets up to the first step, she turns around and sticks her tongue out and heads back into the house. Monica turns back to Damon. "I'm sorry about my sister, for a young girl she has a mouth on her. I swear I don't know who she get it from." Monica laughs. "Its all good she acts like you." Damon replies. "No we are nothing alike she has her own little ways that are no where near mine." Monica exclaimed. "Whatever you say." Damon replies back.

As Damon pulls up to the restaurant Monica looks out of the front window. "Hooters?" Monica questions. "You kidding right?" she questions again. "Nope" Damon gets out of the car and waves for her to come into the restaurant. Monica gets out of the car and Damon says. "Their hot wings are off the chain, you need to try them. I am not lying." As they walk into the restaurant a worker approaches them and shows them to a table. "Can I take your order?" The worker asked. Damon starts telling the waitress his and Monica's order. "We want a order of them hot wings." Any beverages?" she asks. Monica orders a Dr. Pepper and Damon orders sprite.

As the worker walks away Monica looks at her in disgust. "She bet not prepare my meal in them clothes. Her shorts look so tight her juices look like they about to overflow." Damon laughs. "Anyways thank you for coming out tonight with me knowing that you don't get out much." Damon said. "Dude please I get out the house all the time just sometimes I like to be laid back ya know?" Monica said. "So what do you?" Damon questions. "What do you mean what do I do?" She asks. "What do you do for fun?" He questions. "Umm I draw, I play basketball, I do hair, and I do a little free styling." She says. "O that's what's up. I like basketball too; I wanna go into the NBA. Hopefully I'll make it. And you can freestyle huh? Let me hear a lil something." Damon suggested. "Alright alright. Give me a beat." Monica said. "This be ya girl Monica ill as ever, never need dick to prove that I can spit my lyrics stay natural line so sharp I call em suicidal slit ya wrist that's how I make it rain. Oooooo." Monica hollered out. I "Yeah I feel you. You should come see me and my crew down at club Imagination we be shutting down the stage." Damon said. "I'll come one day and see what ya'll can bring no biggie." Monica announced. " Anyways I really wanted you to come with me tonight because I wanted to ask you if you wanted to start talking and if we hit it up you would be my girl soon." he asks. She stares at him as if he has lost his mind. "I just met you yesterday, and you asking me up in hooters. Boy is you out of your mind?" Monica said. "See I been feeling you for awhile and I was afraid to ask you out because you a strong opinionated female and I know you heard about me and my past with the girls saying I'm a cheater which I am not." Damon holds up his hands and shrugs his shoulders. "And what better place to ask." " You could of asked me in the car. And I don't think you a player I can't go by everything people say. I never go by gossip I rather find out for myself but I will be conscious about my every move though you know?" Monica says. Damon smiles "Okay I feel you, so will you?" Monica smiles back looking at Damon's hazel eyes as he winks at her and smiles revealing his one dimple in his left cheek. "Yes I guess I'll go with you, you not too bad your singing was. Especially when we were in the car but other then that you cool." Monica says. "Good, I thought you was going to turn me down." Damon said. "Na, I like you and your sexy dimple." Monica said while laughing. "Thank you." Damon replied.

Around midnight Monique knocks on the door Monica asks. "What do you want?" "Girl open up this door." Monique said. Monica opens up the door " Monique what is you doing here late at night?" she questions. "I just got off from work and I wanted to know how your date went with Damon." "It was good but he took me to hooters." Monica explained. Monique gets even comfortable "Did you try the hot wings?" Monique asks. "Yea" "And?" Monique questions. "He asked me to be his girl." Monique's lower lip drops. "And what did you say?" she asks. Monica rolls her head "I said yes, girl he is to fine to say no and his personality is so damn funny." Monique laughs knowing that she was right about Damon. "Well Monica can you baby-sit Nya tomorrow?" "Yea, no problem I haven't seen my god child since last week." Monica says.

# Chapter 4

## A death in the neighborhood

Monique lays Nya down on the sofa. "Thanks Mo" Monique said. She kisses Nya on her cheek as she lays sleeping. "I'll be back around four." Monica turns on the T.V and walks into the kitchen and takes out the eggs, sausage, biscuits and apples. She starts to cut the apples and stir up the eggs. The aroma rising from the food awakens Nya. She rises up from the sofa and looks around and then looks over to Monica and smiles.

"Morning Nya!" Monica speaks aloud. Nya replies back with a good morning. Then she asks Monica what she is cooking in a sweet delightful voice. "I'm cooking eggs, sausage, fried apples, and biscuits. Are you hungry?" Monica asked. "Yes maam." Nya replies back. Tierra walks up the hallway while rubbing her eyes looking at Monica then turns over towards the living room and hollers out. "Nya!" Nya hollers back "Tierra!" Nya runs over to Tierra and hugs her. "Okay ya'll breakfast is ready." Monica said. Monica turns off the TV and turns on the radio. She fixes both Nya and Tierra's plate.

"O sissy this is my jam." Tierra announced. "I'm to booty luscious for you babe." Singing out in joy. Nya starts to shake her butt. "Nya! What you know about that girl?" Monica asks. She replies back and says "Mommy be dancing to this song." Monica laughs, "I figured." Monica grabs the plates, and cuts off the radio. Tierra bites into the biscuit, which she finds a sweet taste to it. "Sis, what do you have in this biscuit?" She asks. Monica replies back "Jelly." "Jelly? You mean them things in the water? What you trying to do poison me?" Tierra said.

"Shut up Tierra you know exactly what I am talking about you eat it with your peanut butter sandwiches. Don't play with me." "O, It better be." Tierra said. "I love jelly." Nya speaks out. "You do huh?" Monica asks. "Yes, I like them on a pancake its really good. Daddy says it taste just like a jelly filled doughnut." Nya frowns. "That's not quite what I taste when I eat it but it is good." Nya said. Monica laughs, "Your daddy always had an unusual taste bud." "So what do you two want to do today since I'm off from work?" Monica asks. "Can we go shopping?" Tierra asks. "O please? Can we go?" Nya asks. Monica looks at Nya and Tierra. "You two are going to be the cause of me being broke." She says. "So is that a" Nya pauses and gives Monica the puppy eyes. "A yes?" Nya asks. "Yea we can go shopping I need me a new outfit too." Tierra and Nya jump in their chair hollering aloud "We are going shopping!"

Lasha walks out of the house with her baby in her arms to accompany her brother and his friends. "Ya'll want anything to drink." Kim questions. "Some Kool-Aid for Kor'Mayne ma." Lasha speaks out. Kim walks back into the house to get Kor'Mayne's cup. As Lasha continues to walk across the yard a black Cadillac slowly creeps up the street. Music loud the windows tinted. Javar tries to get a glimpse of who was inside. As the car approached the house the window slowly came down smoke rising from the inside of the car. Javar and his friends studied the vehicle closely.

As a head arose from inside of the car Javar was quick to notices that it was one of his own enemies that he had problems with a while back. Quickly drawing out his gun he tells Lasha to get down continuously. But before she could get down eight shots fired as they all hit the ground Javar quickly gets up and starts to fire back at the car but missed and the car speeded off. Javar looks back as he sees two of his friends wounded then looked over towards Lasha and hollers out. "Lasha? Are you and Mayne okay?" There was complete silence he drops his gun and runs over towards Lasha and drops down to the ground. Kim comes outside of the house terrified.

"What's going on out here?" She questions. "What happened? Javar? Lasha?" Kim looks over as she sees Javar's friends wounded. She quickly notices that Javar is crying and holding onto Lahsa and the baby. Kim runs towards them and looks down and covers her mouth and shakes her head screaming "no, not my baby! Not my baby! "Javar call the ambulance! Call the ambulance!" Kim holds the baby tight in her arms and lasha's head lying on her lap rubbing her head. "God please, not my babies!" Neighbors start rushing out of their houses to see what had happened. "Wake up baby! Wake up!" Kim commanded. "Please wake up."

As soon as the ambulance arrived Lasha and Kor'Mayne were already dead. They took the two to the hospital where they were later pronounced dead. That afternoon Monique, Serena, and Neka arrived at Monica's house. "Ya'll I heard there was a shooting that went down in Lasha's neighborhood." There was no reply back "Ya'll where is Lasha at?" a single tear ran down Serena's cheek. "Lasha and her baby were killed in the drive by." Serena announced. "Stop! You lying." "No we're not."

Monica smiles and shakes her head and her expression changes dropping to the floor tears streamed down her cheek dripping off of her chin. Mena walks into the house with Tierra where she notices the four girls on the floor crying. Mena looks and questions, "What is ya'll on the floor for?" Monique looks at Mena and speaks "L and her baby was murdered today." She said. Mena stands in shock. Tierra asks, "Who died mama?" she shakes on her mothers arm. Mena looks down at Tierra and gets on her knees. She looks in her eyes and answers "Lasha, and her baby." "Does that mean they are in heaven now?" she asks. A Mena look down and back up at Tierra and says, "Yes baby, yes."

# Chapter 5

## Revenge

"Lasha was my little girl who always put others before herself. She was one of the most caring and loving daughters I could ever ask for. And my grandson Kor' Mayne always kept a smile on his face just a cheesing except with no teeth. If I could change back time I would. I miss the two of them so much that I cry every night hoping Lasha would come into my room with Kor' Mayne." Jazzabelle said. "Asking me if I could rock him to sleep. Lasha was tired at times from working, school, and being a mother. Her sickness kept her down at times but she never complained. If she was to cry and you was to ask her what's wrong she would always say its just tears of joy." Jazzabelle began to cry. "My baby would never complain she always had a loving heart." Jazzabelle said. She began to cry harder. Javar walked her back to her seat taking his finger and wiping her tears off from her cheeks. As the two coffins slowly went into the ground, family members and friends let loose balloons

In to the air, the preacher announces "May Lasha and Kor'Mayne rest in peace". Javar wipes away his tears and says "Rest in peace, I love ya'll." He drops pink and white roses that Lasha had adored. He walks over to his mother and kisses her. Walking her to the car. "Mama do you need anything while I'm out?" he asks. "No baby I'm fine." She says.

"Okay I'll be back later on." He walks away and drives off. Javar arrives at Dro's house, Lil C, Dro, and Omar gets into the car. Javar looks back and says "I'm ready to get them mother fuckers who did this to my sister and nephew and have no regrets when I'm through with them." As Javar pulls up to the corner he sites Manny and his boys standing on the corner of sixteenth street getting crack and money from prostitutes. As they wait patiently for the three girls to leave, they load up their guns. Javar kisses his cross that was attached to his necklace and looks unto the sky that appeared of a darken orange. "Forgive me." He said. Looking back over as the girls left, Javar starts up his car and drivers slowly up to Manny and his clique.

Lil C hollers out of the window "What it do?" Both sets stare at each other knowing of what is about to happen. Javar nods his head Ace slowly tries to take out his gun from his pants. They all draw out their guns and fired. Lolo, and Ace were dead. Javar jumps out of the car and points the gun towards Manny but Manny begins to run. Javar tries to catch up Manny runs in between two abandoned buildings trying to get away he jumps on the fence and Javar pulls the trigger and shoots Manny's leg. Manny hits the dry cracked concrete; Javar runs up to him and looks down at Manny. Manny begins to laugh and announces "You a pussy ass bitch. If you gonna kill me you should aim better fool."

Manny spits at Javar's shoes. "If you had never touched my girl, maybe your sister would still be alive." Manny said. "I ain't touch that girl man she lied on me. But this aint about her this about what you did." Javar replied back. Manny just looked at Javar "Man, You ain't going to do shit." Manny said. Javar looks at him with hatred and starts to kick Manny's side. As he stops Manny looks at him and laughs as blood runs from his lip. Javar raises his gun at Manny's head. "This is for my sister, nephew, and mama." Javar fires his gun and Manny's head hits the cement. Lil C pulls up to the scene and waves for Javar to get in the car. Lil C hollers out "Come on man the cops are going to be here soon." Javar runs back and jumps into the back seat the car spun off.

That afternoon Monica, and Monique ride's by Lasha's house. As they see Javar is being escorted out of the house in handcuffs while the police is reading him his rights. Monique mummers amongst herself "Damn Javar!" His mother grabs on to the policeman trying to get him off of her son. Javar notices Monica's car and nods his head; the policeman puts Javar into the car and slamming the door. "We got him." The police officer announced on the scanner. Javar's mother touches the window "I'm going to get you out." She says. "Maam step back please?" The officer asks.

Looking at Javar, understanding why he did what he did, but also realizing he took another individuals life. The jury had reached their final decision "On the count of third degree murder Mr. Jose was found not guilty." Javar lets out a sigh of relief. Not guilty he thinks to himself. As the words slowly marinated in his mind he finally realized he had a second chance in living and being free not knowing how he managed to get out of this one. Tears of joy fell from his eyes and rolled down his cheeks. His mother grabs a hold of him pulling him closer hugging him tightly. "Thank you Jesus!" she says aloud in joy. She lets go and the lawyer shakes his hand and says to Javar "keep out of trouble son" Javar responded with a yes sir. He walks out of the courthouse and falls down to his knees looks up to the sky and says "Thank you."

# Chapter 6

## Falling into deep

"Monica, wake up child! You know you have to go to school today" Mena speaks out shaking Monica. "Mmm, Ma I got two more hours before I go to school." Monica mumbles from under her cover. "Girl you need to get your behind up!" Mena walks towards the window and opens up the curtain "Rise and shine sweetheart. Don't make no sense it's so dark in here." Mena slaps Monica's behind. "Get up now." Mena says looking down at her bed she sees Monica's journal. "You still writing ain't you baby?" Mena questioned. "Yeah mama." She says. "You should do something with that and let the world know what you have gone through instead of holding it in especially in a journal baby." Mena says. "I know mama." Mena hits Monica's behind again and smiles "Now get up child." She said and walks out. "Ugh" Monica said. And stumbles out of the bed.

Tierra walks into Monica's room with her facemask on. "Now see you older then me and it don't take me that long to get out of bed." Tierra said. Monica throws a pillow at Tierra and says, "Well at least when I wake up in the morning I don't look like the grinch." Tierra smiles and claps her hands "It's about time you stepped up your jokes." She announces and walks away. Monica gets up off the floor, closes the bathroom door and walks over to the tub to cut the water on.

"Attention students today we are going to share your future careers that you have set for your selves once you have graduated high school." Ms. Jones announced. "O here we go again." Monique mumbles and falls back in her seat. Ms. Jones looks over to Monique. "Monique let's start with you. Looks like you are already in the talking mood." Ms. Jones said. Sitting down she announces, "I want to become a fashion designer." Monique jumps out of her seat and twirls around. "As you can see I love the fashion world but it needs a bit of my feistiness added on to it." "Okay that's interesting Monique. Your personality would show through your designs, very nice choice." "How about you Monica?" Ms. Jones asked.

Monica stands and up and points to herself. "Well… I would like to become an author, and open up my very own business." Monica said. "And what type of business would you like to own?" Ms. Jones questioned. "A club for young teen parents that has no place to go, and is having a hard time with life." Monica said. "That's nice too." Ms. Jones said. "Well class, for our next assignment for the newspaper we need to have surveys, and multiple stories that would interest our readers." "For say, improvements in the school that would better our education, cutest couple, music, and clothes that are in style this year." "We need to capture our readers eye." Ms. Jones explained. "So I would like everyone to have a topic that they would like to write about and report to me what you would like to do."

As the bell rings Monica and Monique heads out of their last class of the day. "Finally!" Monique speaks out. Raising her hands in the air. "What story you planning on doing?" Monique asks. "I don't know yet, I wanna have a story that people want forget about since it's my last year on the newspaper staff." "It's going to take me awhile to think about it. What you planning on writing about?" Monica asks. "The fashion world honey. The do's and don'ts of what to wear and what is hot this year." Monique said. Trey' Shaun walks up to Monique and hugs her flipping Monica's hair. "Boy, this is real hair you don't touch this like you would touch a broad with wonder weave." Monica exclaimed. Trey' Shaun started laughing "My bad shawty."

"Hey Monica I'm going to talk to you later boo." Monique said. "Okay Mo." Monica replied back. As Monica walks down the school steps she notices Damon at the end waiting for her in his car. Monica smiles and says "Hey, baby!" Damon speaks out "Hey, boo!" Monica opens the car door "So how was your day?" Damon questions. "It was good. And yours?" Monica asked. "Mine was good too. I got to work later on today though." Damon said.

As they entered into the house Damon goes over to the refrigerator to grab sodas for Monica and him self. Monica walks over towards Damon and takes the sodas from his hand, looks at him and smiles. Damon smiles back as Monica leans closer to him they fall in to a kiss. She stops and looks at him and shakes her head. Damon starts to shake his head too. Monica laughs and kisses him again. Damon grabs Monica's butt and picks her up as she wraps her legs around his waist. He walks to his room and closes the door. Letting go Monica post up against the wall while Damon stands in front of her.

He continues to kiss her running his hands through her hair. She grabs the bottom of his shirt and slowly pulls it over top of his head. As she throws the shirt on the floor he starts to unbutton her shirt kissing her on her cheek to her neck till he reaches her belly button. His fingers caressed her aching nipples. Monica's head rods back as he unbuttons her pants while he slowly pulled down her panties. Coming back up while Monica stares at him leading him over to his bed. He lies down as she unbuttons his pants. Slowly climbing on top of him she kisses his chest while caressing his penis, slowly stroking him up and down. His eyes rolled around as he licked his lips from the intense sensation. Monica lies on top of him as they switch sides he now lies on top of her. Slowly entering in her as she feels the pain and pleasure of his fourteen and a half inch dick push into her tight pussy. Wrapping her legs around him the muscles in her thighs tighten. Moaning as he continued to ride her trying not to become loud she scream scratching his back till the blood that was once inside him now running on the outside of his back. Riding her in a faster pace he pushes in deeper kissing her lips that had a speck of his ejaculation from giving him head feeling the pressure as he pressed inside of her. She grabs him from behind and pushes him closer to her. Damon kisses her neck as he slowly exits out of her feeling the cool crisp air rush between them as he departs from her warm body. Not able to close her legs she notices Damon had ejaculated wiping the sticky substance off from between her thighs.

"Did you like that baby?" he asks. "Yes, baby I did." She responded. "O shit, baby you bleeding." Monica says. "Damn baby you scratched the shit out of my back." He exclaimed. "My bad." She says. You good he exclaims long as you liked it I'm satisfied. Monica rises up from the bed with the cover wrapped around her. She walks out in to the bathroom and takes a shower. She hollers out from the bathroom. "Damon what time is it?" she asks. "Five." Damon said. "I have to be at work at six. I'm going to need you to take me home so I can get dressed for work." She explained. "Ight." Damon said. He walks into the bathroom to take a shower with Monica. As they finish they quickly get dressed to leave. "Man, I don't feel like going to work today." Monica said. They arrive at her apartment. She leans over to give him a kiss before she gets out. "Talk to you later babe." She said.

# Chapter 7

## Taking her pride

"Damn girl! You living good." Monique announced. Serena looks at her house and turns back to Monique. "What you talking about? She points to the house, and points to the houses down the street. "It's just another house like all the rest of them. Nothing to get excited over." Serena exclaimed. "Why do you like to be in the hood all the time, instead of being here where you don't hear gun shots or see weave pieces in the middle of the street? You must be out your mind." Monique said.

"Girl, it is not all that. My family expects me to become a doctor, or a lawyer and the music we listen to honey." She pauses. "That's whack." Serena exclaimed. "Plus what I look like with one of these preppy boys. No disrespect they cool and everything but I don't want to be dating a dude who takes more time getting dressed then I do. And girl their pants be stuck up their butts and their crouch barely be getting any air." Serena said. "Okay Serena we get the point already." Neka said. Monica and Monique kept laughing to the point where their stomach began to hurt. Serena looks at them and questions "What ya'll laughing for I mean it." "Yea we know." Monica exclaimed. Serena shakes her head "Anyways what ya'll been up to today?" Serena questioned. "Nothing we just got back from shopping."

"O okay." Serena said. "And what about you" Neka asked.

"Ma, making dinner for tonight. Do ya'll wanna come?" Serena asked. "That depends, if you having my macaroni and cheese with the collard greens, and my fried chicken." Monique exclaimed. "I wish. Mama making sardine, with egg rolls, and we going to have a little taste of crystal wine." Monica looks at Serena "What the hell is that." Monica questioned. Serena laughs we eat it every Thursday night she explained. She shrugs her shoulders "It's the usual." "Na girl, I'm okay." Neka said.

They should let me be in that kitchen, I wonder if she would let me cook ya'll dinner tonight." Monique said. Serena says, "Let me ask her. I rather have you make dinner instead of eating that half cooked food she preparing." Serena runs back up to the house. She runs into the family room. "Ma, can my friend cook dinner for us tonight and the family and my friends all eat dinner together?" she asks. "Well darling I don't know." Mrs. Howard said. Serena points out of the window to show her mother her friends. Mrs. Howard looks in shock and covers her chest. "Serena! Those kids darling! Why do you want to have them in our house? Just look at their clothes their low class and you want to welcome them into our home? To cook for us? There is no telling what they might have." Serena slaps her mother, and her mother strikes back

"And to think you out of all people call yourself a Christian, but yet judge others from where they live and look like." Serena looks at her mother and walks out of the house. Monica gets out of the car seeing that Serena is upset and crying. "Serena what's wrong with you girl?" Monica questions. Serena looks at her as she wipes the tears from her face. "My ma is a judge mental bitch. She doesn't have respect for ya'll, she called ya'll ghetto." Serena said. Monique looks in disgust. "Called us what? She better get her facts straight because this here broad has a life of her own and I don't need nobody to put me in no type of category especially somebody who doesn't know me. Please!" Monique said. Neka shakes her head "What's wrong with the world today?" Neka questioned. Monica looks at the window noticing Serena's mother looking out of it. Monica lets go of Serena and walks up to the house and knocks on the door.

"Umm excuse me Mrs. Howard could I have a talk with you?" Monica asked. Mrs. Howard comes out of the house and was quick to say "I never said such a thing my daughter has a mind of her own." Monica looks with curiosity "How did you know I was going to even say that. I could of called you out here to say hi." Monica said. "But since you mentioned it please do tell me what you mean by ghetto." Mrs. Howard waves her hand "Well you know what I mean." She said. Monica looks at Mrs. Howard "No I don't know. That's why I'm asking you." Monica said. "O, I'll tell you what she meant." Monique said while walking up to the house. "What she was trying to say was that we ain't nothing but trash. Just a bunch of low class kids from the block who don't have anything to do with their lives and who doesn't belong in this type of neighborhood. That's what she was trying to say." Monique announced.

"How dare you insult me like that." Mrs. Howard said. "Insult you? How dare you insult me and my friends like that!" Monica said. "Yea we are from the ghetto but that don't make us ghetto. We are our own individual and we don't settle for nothing less we are smart, intelligent, caring, confident, and faithful." Monica said. "So until you really know us don't you dare judge us. Because if you have not notice we are the future and Mrs. Howard we are making a difference." Monica exclaimed.

Mrs. Howard looks astound. "Well I'm truly sorry for what I said. I didn't mean to hurt you by it." Monica looks at Mrs. Howard "Mrs. Howard I want to believe what you have just said but right now it looks like you are trying to play the victim." Monica exclaims and walks away. They all get into the car even Serena and drives off.

"I can't believe that woman man." Monique said. "I know that's why I'm moving with my dad." Serena exclaimed. "Is your father cool Rena?" Neka asks. " Yea he cool, he is the best thing that has happened in my life he was there for me when I needed him the most. That's my backbone." Serena announced. "That's good I wish I had a father figure like that in my house hold." "What can I say my ma has been both a mother and a father to me and my bro." Neka said. "Yea my pops died from cancer when I was fourteen." Monica announced. "I was a little daddy's girl, but when he passed everything went down hill. My family was in debt for awhile, no water we had to buy jugs of water and boil it to make it hot just to bathe, and sometimes we went days without food; it was hard." "My mother never turned to prostitution, or drugs. Thank you Jesus. She took care of us like a mother should had." Monica said. "Well my mom walked out on me like her ma walked out on her and I always prayed that I would never turn out that way with my daughter, it always worried me when I was pregnant. How could they leave something so precious? But my daddy has token care of my three brothers and me and him battling with diabetes it ain't no joke he gets sick often. He always talks about death, like it's something necessary to say, and he always carries a mean look on his face. Trey' Shaun was afraid to meet him at first but when I had gotten pregnant he had no choice but to meet him." Monique announced. "And once he met him they been best buds since." Monique started laughing. "Ugh they just talk and talk and talk." Neka laughs and announces "My grandpa set his underwear on the couch when C.J had to meet him. It was the most hilarious, and embarrassing thing he could ever do." Neka said. They all began to laugh.

"See you tomorrow Neka." Monica said. Neka walks into the house and turns around and waves back. Monica drives Serena back home. Serena looks out of the window "I see my ma is not home yet." She exclaimed. "Yep." Monica replied. "Alright Monica I'll talk to you tomorrow girl." Serena announced. "Okay. See you later boo" Monica said. Monica drives off as Serena walks to her house she notices her door is halfway open. She slowly opens the door up to check inside. Serena quickly calls the cops as she runs to the kitchen to get a knife. She hears a noise and looks back but see nothing. "911, what is the emergency?" the worker asked. "Hello! Hello! Can you hear me?" Serena asks. "Maam please talk clearly and tell us what is wrong." The worker said. "There has been a break in at my house." Serena said. "Maam where do you live?" the worker asked while trying to keep calm. The signal started to break up. "Maam? Are you there?" she asked. Serena tries to answer her question but loses signal. The worker notices the call was lost and looks for the location where the call had token place. "Get line four on this emergency call to six ninety five Lakewood Drive." The worker commanded. She mumbles amongst herself "Hang in there child." Serena hears the noise again and looks back and says, "I called the cops!" As she walks back to the front door trying to get out of the house, she hears another noise but it sounds closer to her she turns around and a man grabs her and pulls her over to the couch while covering her mouth. "Don't you make a sound, or I'll kill you." The man said. Serena tries to stab him but he grabs a hold of her hand.

"Little lady, what is you trying to do there?" he asks. Serena screams for help but he tells her to keep quite. He starts to touch and unbuttons her blouse. Serena screams no aloud. But he just keeps on.

Serena lies down on the couch hopeless. The sirens of the police car frighten the robber and he run towards the back door. Serena rises from the couch and pulls up her panties and buttons her blouse. The police run into the house and questions. "Maam are you okay?" she asks while looking around she finds Serena sitting on the floor rocking back and forth crying. The other policemen runs into the living room shining their light around. The light lands on Serena "Maam are you okay." The police ask her. Serena shakes her head no. The police picks Serena up and takes her to their car. "Maam could you tell me exactly what happened tonight?" The lady asks her. The police notice handprints around Serena's neck and the prints around her wrist. "Maam would you please tell me where you got these hand prints on you from?" The police lady asked. Serena looks at her but is too terrified to talk.

She calls the ambulance. "Maam we are going to take you to the hospital so you can get examined. Okay?" The lady said. "And my name is Sandra Haults by the way." Serena looks at her "My name is Serena." She said. "Serena Howard." "Well Serena you are in good hands." Serena shakes her head "Okay." She said.

"Hello!" Monica said. "Monica, could you come to the hospital please?" Serena asked. "Yea sure what's wrong?" Monica questioned. "I've been raped." Serena said. Monica drops the phone. "O my god." Monica said she picks the phone back up. "I'll be there in ten minutes you hang in there okay." She said. Serena replied back with an okay. Damon and Monica leave her apartment to go to the hospital. Monica sees Serena getting her mouth swabbed and runs to the room. "O, Serena I am so sorry." Monica said. "It wasn't your fault." She says. Monica hugs Serena and sees a cop walk by. She runs up to the cop and points into his face and says. "I want you to find the bastard who did this to my friend." And then she walks away. "Monica calm down!" Damon said. "How the hell can I calm down when there is a man out there who raped and beat my friend and these people in whom they call their selves policeman say that they are doing the best they can. When they are sitting here on their asses doing nothing." Monica exclaimed. "Stop Monica, they are doing everything they can to find this man." Damon said. "I can't." she gets even louder. "How can somebody be so low to do something like this? I already lost one I don't need to lose another." Monica exclaimed then she stops and puts her hand on her forehead and stumbles on to the ground and passes out. Damon grabs

Monica "Monica are you okay." Monica looks at Damon but her vision is blurry.

"Ms. Branketon, Hi I'm Dr. Johnson and you had an accident last night. You had stumbled on the floor. We checked you out and we found out that you are six weeks pregnant." You were dehydrated at the time. Did you know that you was pregnant?" The doctor asked. "No, no I didn't" Monica said. "Where is Serena?" Monica asked. Ms. Howard is in her room laying down getting rest, the same thing that you need to be doing." The doctor exclaimed. Monica looks at the doctor "Where is Damon?" she asked. "He went out for awhile." The doctor said. "I'm pregnant?" Monica asks. "Yes maam, you are." The doctor said. Damon walks in the room with breakfast and flowers. "Good Morning baby." Damon said. Monica smiles and Damon leans over to kiss Monica. "Morning boo." Monica replied back. "Well I will leave you two alone and I will come back in a little while." Dr. Johnson said. "So baby you doing alright?" Damon asked.

"Yea, I'm doing better. But." Monica said. "But what?" Damon asked. " But I got some news from the doctor." Monica said. "And what is that news?" Damon asked. She looks at Damon and starts to twiddle with her fingers "Baby, I'm six weeks pregnant." "Your what?" Damon asks again. "I'm six." Holding up her fingers. "I'm six weeks pregnant."

Damon looks around in shock "You?" pointing to Monica then pointing to himself "Me?" "Baby?" he asks. Monica smiles "Yea." She says. "Wow." He exclaims. "I'ma be a daddy!" he starts to tear up "I'ma be a daddy." He repeats. "Are you excited?" she asks. "Yea I'm excited. I got you and a baby on the way." He explained. Monica smiles. "Did they get Serena's rapist?" she questions. "Yep, they caught him last night. It was one of her neighbors. He had robbed a liquor store that night too." Damon explained. Monica lets out a sigh of relief. "I want to go see her." She said. "Ight, but what about your rest you need." Damon said. "That can wait, I wanna see my home girl." Monica said. Monica gets down off of the bed and Damon walks her to Serena's room she knocks on the door. "Yea?" Serena said. "Can I come in?" Monica asked. "Yea, sure." Serena said. Monica comes in "So how are you holding in all of this?" Monica asked. Serena looks down "I'm still a little shaken up but I'm okay now that I know they caught him." Serena said. "That's good." Monica said. "Yea, I'm ready to stand trial. And put him away for good." Serena said. Monica grabs a hold of Serena's hand " Yea and I will be with you every step of the way." She exclaims. "Thank you Monica." Serena said. "No problem girl, we stick together in situations like this." Monica exclaims. Monica smiles.

"Will everybody rise?" The policeman says. The judge walks up to her seat. And Serena is in the stand. "Do you swear to tell the truth the whole truth and nothing but the truth so help you god." The clerk asks. "I do" Serena replied. "Ms. Howard would you please tell us what happened on Friday night on April fifth two?" The lawyer asks. "I had just been dropped off at my house that night after being with my friends that afternoon. And I walked up to the house and noticed that my door was open and my ma wasn't at home at that time. So I went inside and looked and I called the police I went into the kitchen and grabbed a knife and I heard noise so I hollered and said I called the police. As I walked out of the house I heard a noise and it was getting louder." Serena explained. "And then he came up behind me and told me if I had screamed he would kill me." Serena started to cry. "He unbuttoned my pants and took off my shirt and was kissing on me." I said no, but he just kept going and I tried to stab him but he pulled the knife away from me." "I tried I really tried, and that's when he raped me." Serena explained. "Ms. Howard wasn't it dark at the time?" The lawyer asked. "Yes." Serena replied. "So how was you able to identify Mr. Kise?" She asked. "Well first off it sounded like him, and when he use to come over my house to see my ma he always told me stories and one of those stories was how he got his scar on his left arm from when he fell and hit his arm on the metal part on his boat." I had seen the scar that night and I got a glimpse of his face. As a shining from the pole light came through the window." Serena said. "That will be all your honor."

"On behalf of the jury we find Mr. Kise guilty of rape/ and sexual abuse, and armed robbery." The jury said. "Mr. Kise you will be facing thirty-four years in prison without bail." "Court-dismissed." Serena looks back as her mother cries and reaches for a hug. "I'm so sorry baby, I am so sorry." Ms. Howard said. "It's okay ma." Serena says. Serena's father comes up behind and hugs her tightly. Monica, Neka, Damon, Trey' Shaun, and Monique looks at Serena and smiles. "You did it girl!" Monique hollers out. Serena runs to them and they all hug her one at a time. “We love you Serena.” Neka said. “Yea Serena we do.” Monica said.

# Chapter 8

## Finally Speaking

As Monica unlocks the door Damon kisses her walking into the apartment they find Mena sitting on the couch watching TV with Tierra accompanying her. Mena looks at them. "Hey baby. Hey Damon" Mena says. "Hey ma, Hi Mrs. Branketon." Both Damon and Monica say. "What you two been up to lately?" she questions.

"We were at Serena's court hearing." Monica replied. As they walk over towards the couch. "What happened? Did he get prison time?" Mena asked. "Yea he got thirty-four years." Mena smiles. "That's good.," she said. "Mhm." Monica shakes her head. "Ma?" Monica said. "Yes baby." Mena said. Monica looks at Damon and rubs his leg and looks back up at her ma. "I'm pregnant." She said.

Mena sits in shock "Say what? I know I didn't hear what I thought I just heard. Monica baby? You pregnant?" she asks. "Yes maam." Monica replies back. "Damon and Monica why didn't you two have protected sex?" Mena questioned. "We was caught up at the moment and was not really thinking about using a condom." Damon replied. "Ma? Damon and Monica had sex?" Tierra asked. Mena looks at Tierra "Girl, if you don't get your butt in your room." Mena said.

"See now ya'll never tell me what's going on. But I got ya'll, I got you." Tierra said. Tierra starts to walk in her room and shuts the door as she hears them still talking she opens up the door slowly so she could hear more. "Baby, are you sure you are pregnant?" she asks. "Yes, maam. The doctor had told me that day I was at the hospital with

Serena." Monica explained. "Does that mean I'm going to be a auntie?" Tierra asked. "Tierra stay out of this!" Mena said. "Why didn't you two come to me or call me once you found out?" Mena questioned. "Me and Damon had to talk about it first of all." Monica explained. Mena shakes her head.

"Well you two are going to keep this baby. I didn't abort you or Tierra. And I expect for you not to abort either. You hear me?" Mena said. "Yes, maam but I, no we wouldn't abort our baby no matter what." Monica said. "Good, and I want ya'll to finish school too. Just because this situation has occurred doesn't mean that you have to quit school" Mena exclaimed. "Yes maam and Mena I love Monica so much. Sometimes I feel like I'm smothering her from loving her to much." Damon said. "Damon you can never love someone too much." Mena said. Damon shakes his head up and down. "Damon have you told your mother about this?" Mena asks. Damon shakes his head.

"No, she is never around for me to tell her anything. She's on cocaine so the only time me or my little brother and my little sister are able to see her is when she comes home to make her a sandwich and she barely does that and I don't want to tell her that she can't eat the food at our place because then Lala and Chris won't ever see her." Damon replied. She looks sick you can see her spine from her back. I don't know what to do" Damon said. "Well baby when you do see her I want you to tell her. Sit her down and tell her how you feel, don't you let her go until you tell her everything. Okay?" "Yes, maam." Damon says. Mena leans over to Damon and Monica and hugs them. "I love ya'll." She announced. "I love you too." Damon and Monica said.

"Let go of the remote control!" Lala commands. "No, it's my turn to watch TV." Chris said. Damon walks into the living room. "Lala give him the remote control you've already had your turn." Lala hands Chris the remote control and flips her hair. "I'm a lady you know, we should always get our way." Lala said. "Yea you are a lady, but you also need to learn how to share." Damon announced. Lala folds her arms "He is such a crybaby, I'm going into my room and put my makeup on. A diva always needs to look good." "I'm already beautiful but I love makeup." Lala announced. Damon kisses the two and walks back into his room.

Rose walks into the house over towards the kitchen dressed in dingy clothes that hung off her shoulders and sagged off her butt. "Mommy,

mommy!" Lala and Chris holler out. They run up to their mother and give her a hug. "O, my goodness ya'll have grown up so fast." Rose said. "Mommy when are you going to come back home and stay?" Lala asked. "Well Lala I don't know when I'ma come back." Rose exclaimed and changes the subject. "Umm are ya'll doing okay?" She asks. "Yea, me and Lala got A, B honor roll in school. The teacher said that we are very smart kids." Chris said.

"That's good baby that's good." Rose looks around and asks. "So where is your brother?" "He's in his room." Lala said. Rose runs her fingers through Lala's hair "Okay, mommy is going to fix a quick bite to eat and leave okay. I don't want you to make a sound alright?" Rose looks at her two kids. "Okay?" she says. Chris and Lala cover their mouth shaking their head.

As Rose heads to the door Damon comes up the hallway surprised and asks, "Where are you going?" Rose pauses and looks down at the floor and back up she rubs her hands together and turns around. "Hi baby." Rose said. "Hi ma, so where are you going?" Damon asks. "Damon why you always ask that baby?" she questions. "Because I just want to know. So where are you going?" He questions again. "I'm just going out for a walk." She says. "A walk huh? You going out just for a walk right?" He walks up to her. "Mama you always say your going out for a walk, you have been saying that for the past year I'm not a child anymore so you can stop talking to me like I am one." "I know what you do. I saw you on the street dealing drugs, and getting into some stranger's car. People who you don't even know." You rather choose drugs, and men over your own children. Your own flesh and blood." Damon said. She slaps him he rubs his cheek. "Don't you ever talk to me like that. Boy I put my life on hold for ya'll. I took care of ya'll, loved ya'll, I been there for ya'll through thick and thin. And you are going to come at me with this non-sense. When are ya'll going to be there for me? See you owe me I gave birth to you" Rose speaks out.

"How can you call yourself a mother? Did you know that Lala and Chris are the top five A, B honor roll students in their grade level? Did you know that I got a scholarship for basketball? Did you know that?" "See you never took the time to sit down and find these things out." "They sat up all night crying with the stomach virus and who was there to care for them? Me. Who brought in the food, paid the electricity bill, the water bill, and the rent? Me. Who became both the mama and father for the both of them? Me. It was me mama. Me." Damon speaks out he starts to cry. I stayed in school when all daddy wanted me to do was drop out and work like him. I'm not going to be stuck on welfare with kids and my girlfriend. I want better for myself. I can't repeat what you and him did it ended you two no where."

"Why can't you just be there for us? I want you to be there for Lala, and Chris. I want you to see me on graduation day and tell me that you are proud of me. I want you to be there when my baby is born. I want you to be there. No I don't want you to I need you to." Damon speaks out. Rose starts to cry she wipes the tears from Damon face as she hears the horn beep from a car. "I'm sorry I have to go." She closes the door behind her.

"Attention class it's a brand new day. And I hope over the weekend ya'll thought about your assignment." Ms. Jones. "I'ma call on everybody and I want you to tell me your topic that you are going to write about for the last school newspaper starting with you Jalisa." Ms. Jones announced. "Well this school is my topic. I'm going to write about the improvements that need to be made. But I'm going to put a twist to it and I want to write about what would make learning more fun." Jalisa explained.

"Good, make sure you make it to where when the reader turn the page it captures their eye. That goes for all of ya'll." "Monica how about you?" She asks. Monica just stares at Ms. Jones she squints her eyes huh? She asks. "What is the topic of your paper?" As Monica runs out of the classroom feeling dizzy and nausea. "Monica? Monica? Where are you going?" Ms. Jones questioned. She runs after her and when she opens up the bathroom door she hears Monica throwing up. She holds Monica's hair back. "It's okay." She exclaimed "Pregnant huh?" Ms. Jones questioned. Monica shakes her head and starts to throw up again. "Yea I had a feeling you was. It's going to be okay." "You need something to eat and some water?" she asks. Monica shakes her head no and wipes her mouth. "O god, eww I just did that?" Monica asks Ms. Jones. Ms. Jones laughs "Yea you did."

"Monica what happened girl?" Neka asked. "I'm sick Neka I just want to go home." Monica said. "Making sure, have you ate yet?" Neka asked. "I can't when I look at food I get even sicker." Monica replied. "Monica you need to go to the doctor and find out what's wrong."

Neka suggested. "I have and I'm pregnant that's the only reason why I'm feeling like this." Monica said. "Monica, you pregnant?" Neka questioned. Monica shakes her head "Yes." Monique walks down the hall hollering in the hallway. "What it is people?" Monica and Neka turn around "O lord here come big mouth." Monica exclaimed. Neka laughs "Yep that's her alright." "Hey boo's what ya'll up to?" Monique questions. "Just talking." Neka replied. "Monica what you up to?" She questions. "I just got finished telling Neka that I'm pregnant." Monica said. Monique backs away "Ms. Branketon pregnant? Get out of here. Are you serious?" Monique said. "Yea." Monica replied. "Aww congratulations girl." Monique announced. "Thanks. I'ma get at ya'll later." Monica said.

Mena sites Damon's mother at the corner of the liquor and pulls over "Ms. McIntosh how are you I'm Monica's mother Mena." Rose looks at her strangely. "Do I know you or something?" Rose questions. "No you don't but Damon is my daughter's boyfriend." Mena explained. "O, yea he told me that. I just didn't know her name. So she pregnant right?" Rose asks. "Yea, she is and I would appreciate it if you would be there during labor, and for Damon's graduation." Mena said. "I don't know if I can do that I'm very busy." Rose said. "Well let me give you my number." Mena suggested. Mena gets out a pen from her purse and writes her number on the palm of Rose's hand. "Alright you got my number please do call sometimes." Mena said. Rose shakes her head and walks off and joins a crowd of women. Mena looks as Rose walks away "Lord, bless the lost soul, and let it find the light again." Mena said.

"Sis, when you have the baby will you still have time for me?" Tierra asks. Monica looks at Tierra and tilts her head to the side. "Yea, I'll make time. Why you ask that?" Monica questions. "Nothing just asking, and I'ma have time for you too big sis." Tierra said. Monica looks at Tierra "You have no choice Tierra, all you doing is going to school and your little dance team. It's not like you go to school, work, and pregnant like me." Monica explained. "I know but I stay busy for a five year old." Tierra said. "Uh huh." Monica mumbled. Tierra walks over to Monica and gives her a hug Monica hugs back. "I love you sis!" Tierra said. "I love you too!" Monica replied. "Okay now you messing up the hair." Tierra said. Monica lets go of Tierra, "What are you going to name your baby?" Tierra asked. "If it is a girl her name will be Kaleena Akira Johnson, and if it's a boy his name will be Faizon Jermell Johnson." Monica exclaimed. "I like that." Tierra said. "I bet you do." Monica exclaimed.

# Chapter 9

## A miracle

"These nine months have been something else for me especially being pregnant with triplets." Monica exclaimed. "Yea I know how you feel it was the same thing for me except the stuff that then happen this year has been crazy and you having three kids that's wild." Monique said. "Yea I hope I will become a good mother." Monica said. "O, don't even worry bout that you will be a good mother. You smart, pretty, funny, and you work your ass off to get what you want." Monique explained. Monica listens to Monique carry on with her conversation but is in pain and trying to keep her balance. "Why Monique such nice words." Monica laughs. "Naw thanks girl." Monica said.

Monica leans down in pain and screams "Mo! My water broke!" she hollered out. "O hell!" Monique said. "Can we get some help over here my friend is pregnant!" Monique hollers out. Monique wraps Monica's arm around her neck, two men runs up to them and picks Monica up and Monique walks with them to the car. "Thank you." Monique said. "You are welcome maam." The two men said. She buckles the seatbelt around Monica. "Hold on girl. Don't you have no baby in here!" Monique exclaimed. As Monique is rushing to the hospital she calls Damon, Mena, Neka, Serena, and Trey' Shaun. "Get to the hospital ASAP Monica is having her baby." Monique exclaimed.

"Maam, I'ma need you to breath for me, and relax." The doctor said. She looks at the doctor and gives her a mean face. "I am breathing doc, and I can't relax how can I relax there is no relaxing in this situation it's too painful to relax." Monica said while screaming and shouting. Damon smiles at Monica "I'm here baby, you got this ight." Damon said.

Monica pushes giving birth to her baby boy then her baby girl comes out shortly after the first birth. "I don't think I can push anymore." Monica said. Touching her chest "I can't breath!" she exclaimed. Monica tries to catch her breath but is unable to. Monica starts to sweat excessively she starts to push regardless of the fact she couldn't hardly breath as her son was delivered Monica passes out. "Monica! Wake up!" Damon commanded shaking her. He starts to cry, "Please get up!" Mena, Tierra, Monique, Neka, Serena, Lasha

And Trey' Shaun runs into the room. "What's going on?" Mena asked. She looks at Monica "What's wrong with her?" she questions. "Maam will you please step outside." The doctor said. "No, not until you tell me what's wrong!" Mena commanded. Tierra yanks on her mother's arm "Mommy what's wrong with sissy?" she asks. Monica's heart rate starts dropping and soon it went into a flat line. The doctor rushes to Monica as assistant's runs into the room to attend to the situation that has occurred. Mena stands at the doorway looking into the room crying.

Damon hits the wall as Monique comforts him "It will be okay." she says. The doctor gives Monica an electric shock. Her heart rate starts beating but goes back into a flat line the doctor shakes his head. Mena looks into the room and sees that the doctor has given up she hollers from outside of the room and says "Don't you let my baby die, don't you dare give up on her!" she commanded. The doctor looks at her and looks down at Monica then looks at the other nurse and shakes his head up and down. His assistance tells him to try one more time. The doctor shocks her Monica's heart rain starts beating again the doctor looks at the monitor and wipes his forehead he looks at Mena and walks out into the hallway. He moves his hands around "She is okay, she needs a lot of rest, and oxygen." He explains. "O, thank God." Mena said. Damon looks up with Tierra in his arms he wipes his tears away and takes a deep breath he looks up and says "Thank you."

The next two days Mena walks into the room with Tierra and Damon. "Hey beautiful." Mena said. "Hey mama." Monica replied back. Mena walks towards Monica and kisses her on her forehead. Damon walks in with flowers while Tierra is holding balloons; Tierra runs and jumps on Monica's bed "Sissy, I'm glad you're okay. You had me worried." Tierra said. "I did huh? I told you I wasn't going to leave you." Monica exclaimed. Monica looks over to Damon "Hey boo." She said. "Hey Baby." He replied back. He walks over to give her a hug. "Where my babies at?" she asks. "They in the nursery room, two boys and a girl." Damon said. "Yep, there beautiful, and healthy." Mena said. "I wanna see them." Monica exclaimed.

Monica looks through the glass as she sees her triplets "Aww they are adorable." Tierra announced. As the nurse brings her babies to Monica she starts to cry. "Kaleena Akira, Isaiah Ronald, and Faizon Jermell Johnson." Monica announced. "We made some sexy babies." Damon said. Monica laughs "We sho did."

As Monica's babies are sleeping in their crib Monica is typing on her computer "Honey, what are you up to?" Mena asked. Monica shuts her computer off quickly. "Umm nothing just doing a little research." She exclaimed. "Uh huh, are you hungry?" Mena asked. "Yeah." Monica replied. As Mena walks out of the room Monica cuts back on her computer and lets out a big sigh of relief and starts to type again.

"Hello, class I have some good news." Ms. Jones announced. "We have sold over a thousand copies of the school newspaper." She said. Every one starts to applaud. "Yes, I am very happy for ya'll. You have showed your talents through this. From the artwork to the paper work you have aced it all. I couldn't be more proud of this class." Ms. Jones said. "I appreciate your hard work and time that you have put into every story in the school newspaper. Thank you." Ms. Jones announced. Monica walks in the classroom. "Umm Ms. Jones I have something I would like to give to you." Monica hands Ms. Jones a stack of papers. "Monica what is this for?" She asked. "Well Ms. Jones I thought about what you had offered me. And my father before he passed away always sat me down and said to me Monica I want you to show the world your talents, don't you ever give up on something. If you want it bad enough I want you to work your hardest to get it. Don't try to take the easy way out. See the light through all of the troubles and let it guide you. So Ms. Jones I have written this essay not only for me, not only for my children's, not for my man, not only for my sister or mother, but for my father." Though he may be gone a piece of him still lives in me, and that is my heart. So I would like to enter this into the contest." Monica exclaimed.

Ms. Jones looks at Monica and sheds a tear "Good, I am so taken away by your courage you are an inspiration Monica. And I thank you for that." Ms. Jones said. Monica smiles "No, thank you Ms. Jones." Monica hugs Ms. Jones and whispers "Thank you."

# Chapter 10

## Papa was right

"I'm so nervous." Neka exclaimed. "Me, too I can't stand being in front of a big crowd." Serena replied. The principal stands on stage looking upon the audience and announces. "Welcome to Crenshaw High's graduating class of two-thousand and nine." "I am proud to say that we have an outstanding group of young ladies and gentlemen in this year's class that has done a wonderful job in their attendance, and their work in school." "Not only that but also their positive attitudes they have in and out of school. They are the future; I would also like to acknowledge our contest winner for the short story essay."

"She was nominated as the first grand prize winner in the city. May we all applaud Ms. Monica Branketon as she accepts this scholarship and her very own contract with The Future Publishing Company." The principal announces. Monica walks up to accept her scholarship and signs the contract with the publishing company. "I would like to thank everyone that has believed in me even when I didn't believe in myself this is a true blessing. And I would like to thank Ms. Jones for pushing me to do this and for my father who encouraged me to never give up and my mother, my sister, my man, my triplets, and my friends without ya'll there is no me. I love you. And I also wanted to say papa was right." Monica announced.

Everyone in the audience applauds as Monica finishes speaking, then the principal walks back on the stage. "I will now announce our senior's class of two-thousand and nine. Mr. Damon Johnson. A varsity football, basketball, and baseball player who has received a scholarship for basketball at NCU." The principal said. "Damon baby!" Damon turns around and looks into the audience Monica turns around in her seat. Damon see's his mother.

"Damon, I love you! Go ahead with your bad self!" Rose hollers out while standing holding both Chris and Lala. Damon smiles as tears of joy rolls down his face. Monica smiles at her mother, Mena winks at Monica. "Thank you." Monica said. "Mr. Jerone Winterson. A varsity football player." The principal announces again. After every student had received their diploma they all threw their caps into the air celebrating. Rose runs to Damon. "I'm sorry baby, I am sorry. I love you and I am very proud of you." She said and hugs him tightly. "I love you too mama." Damon speaks. Mena rubs Monica's cheeks. "Congratulations baby." She said. "Thanks ma." Monica holds two of her babies as Damon holds the other. Monique and Trey' Shaun walks up with their baby. Then Neka and C.J walked up with their baby, and Serena approaches them with her new boyfriend.

"Everyone I would like ya'll to meet my boyfriend Rick." Serena announced. "Hi Rick." Monica said. "Hey." He replied back. "Welcome to the family." Monique greeted.

"Man, we men now." Trey' Shaun says to Damon and C.J. C.J points to the girls. "Yea, man and look at our women." C.J replied. "Yup, we got the best." Damon said. Rose gathers up everybody. "Okay now everyone say cheese on the count of three." Rose said. Rick backs away so he wouldn't be in the picture. "Boy get in this picture." Mena said. "You sure?" Rick asked. "Yea, you apart of the fam now." C.J said. Rick stands beside Serena. "Alright now One two." The light from the camera flashes. "Nice." Rose said.

"So Monica what was that essay about?" Neka asked. Monica smiles "It was about us. That little black journal I always had everything that happened between me and the things that happened to my home girls I wrote about it and I dedicated it to us." She said.

"O ain't that sweet, you know you so sweet. Sweeter then honey." Monique said. "Come on ya'll we have a hour to get you all to your baptism." Mena said. Rose announces I am getting baptized with you all too, it's time to support my family time for me to be there and change my life around and to never look back." She said. Damon smiles and hugs his mother tighter. "Thank you mama." He whispers in her ear.

Five years later Monica has became an author selling over five million copies of her book, and has opened up her very own nail and hair salon, with a soul food restaurant beside it. Damon is now a pro basketball player and has his very own business for people who are on drugs seeking for help. Neka is a professional photographer. C.J and Trey' Shaun are music producers. Serena is a speaker for rape victims and is currently pregnant with her boyfriend Rick's baby. And Monique is acting.

"Baby where is you going?" Damon asked. "You'll see." She said. Monica pulls up to the graveyard. "Wait here." She said.

Monica sits down on the ground and lays roses against the gravestone and begins to speak. "Lasha, boo the times you made us laugh, and smile was the days. You always said I was the goofy one of the group but nah girl you was the goofiest, and whenever we was sad you would take us by the hand and tell us that everything would be okay even though you was going through a tough time yourself you tended not to let it bother you. Girl you was a soldier no not a solider but a survivor you battling with AIDS and being a single parent." Monica pauses as a tear falls down her cheek. "How did you do it? Girl I know you in heaven like dang chica what you crying for? I know you better wipe them tears away. But girl you don't know how much I miss you."

Monica looks up to the sky. We all miss you. You brought light to the room it want ever be the same with out you. I love you Lasha." Monica said. Monica kisses her hand and lays it on top of the gravestone, and walks back to the car. As Monica's daughter questions "Mama! Can we go get some ice cream?" Monica smiles and answers, "Yea, we can go get some ice cream." Kaleena smiles back. "Mommy who was you talking to?" Isaiah asks. "A friend." Monica looks up to the sky. "A very good friend." "Mommy I love you!" Faizon said with excitement. "I love you too boo." Monica replied. As Monica drives off an angel stands beside the gravestone with a baby in its arms they both blow a kiss and disappears. "So what ya'll want to do today?" Monica questioned. "Well first mommy we want some ice cream then we wanna go see a movie, then we wanna go to the park, then we wanna go to grandma's, then we wanna." Faizon, Kaleena, and Isaiah said. "Ya'll just wanna go every where today huh?" Monica said. "Yes maam." The three of them replied. “Well we going to go get some ice cream first.” Damon said. Monica looked at him “You always encouraging them to eat sweets.” She said. “Baby I got this.” Damon said. “Mhm when they stomach be hurting from them sweets ima say goodnight and go to sleep while you take care of their stomach ache.” Monica said. Monica looks over to her kid’s smiles and says. “I love ya’ll.”

# In Between the Two

In Between the Two is a story about a twenty-two year old by the name of Jazz' Rae. Jazz' Rae is a young lady who had moved from Virginia to Atlanta so that she could get away from the life of the streets, watching her back every five minutes was not her ideal of a good life. Starting as a brand new person at a new location wasn't hard for her. She had the looks that scored well with the guys, and the attitude that told girls to keep their distance. She met Nunu at her current job at the daycare and been friends with her ever since. Jazz' Rae was not use to females she hung around the guys more because in her mind females were nothing but a lot of mouth and drama. After meeting Nunu Jazz' Rae partied and came up upon Ker'Shaun a slick talking player that was well known for hustling and for being a ladies man. Jazz' Rae seemed not to let the rumors bother her until she found him with another girl. After a two-year relationship things had all come to an end. She was fed up with the lies from guys; she made a promise to not jump into the next relationship with a guy right after meeting him. Shortly after the breakup she begins to concentrate more on herself, and getting back into the single life again was not easy.

She is like a baby still attached to the umbilical cord when dealing with the single life. She's so use to receiving phone calls and knocks at her door late at night. Being cooped up with just one person and knowing she has a significant other that is there to comfort her. Just as she starts to get used to this new life everything clashes. Her friend puts her up for a blind date while shopping out and not knowing what to expect of this mysterious person Jazz' Rae is nervous and curious at the same time. When the date goes well she and the gentleman began to talk and later becomes involved. But her ex soon re-appears back into her life. Though she has gotten involved with someone else she is still in love with her ex. Not knowing what to do Jazz' Rae is stuck in between the two.

# Chapter One-

## Lust Conquers All

Sniffing the air she smells an unusual aroma puckering up her nose she follows the scent noticing it's the smell of hot sex. As she reaches the end of the hall she hears a loud moaning; taking the knob and lifting the door up a little to keep it from making noise she opens it to find her man Ker'Shaun on top of another girl pounding against her. "O hell naw!" Jazz' Rae shouted stomping her foot on the floor. "I know you don't have no trifling ass bitch in my bed." She pointed to herself waiting for an answer. Ker'Shaun gets up from in between the girl "Who the fuck are you and why are you talking to my man like that?" The girl questioned while sliding out of the bed holding the cover close to her naked body. Looking for her panties that were scattered on the floor with the rest of her clothing she spots them quickly picking them up. "Yo man?" Jazz' Rae looks around. "Bitch you up in my bed with my man in between your legs." Jazz' Rae shouted while on the other side of the room. "Ker'Shaun! Who the fuck is this?" The girl pointed and questioned in anger. Jazz' Rae began taking off her earrings putting them into her front pocket of her dark denim jeans taking off her heels Ker'Shaun holds out his hands and speaks. "Baby, baby calm down it's not what you think." Ker'Shaun said. Jazz' Rae lifts up her heel. "If it's not what I think then why in the hell am I about to whoop you and this lil bitches ass?" She questions. She turns around to notice that the girl is trying to get out from the fire escape onto the rusty ladders that were barely strong enough to hold her. Running over Jazz' Rae grabs her by her hair and began beating the broad in the head. The girl throws her hand up cuffing it up under Jazz' Rae's chin to push her back. "Don't be putting your hands in my face bitch." Jazz' Rae said while continuing to beat her. Pulling away the girl finally manages to get from Jazz' Rae and began heading down the ladder half undressed. From pulling away Jazz' Rae was able to grab a handful of the girl's hair. She hollers out from the window "Bitch next time it won't be just the tracks!" she shouted throwing the hair out the window. Ker'Shaun grabs hold of Jazz' Rae "Calm down man." He said while kissing her neck. As Jazz' Rae lowers her tone she jerks away from Ker'Shaun "Get up off of me." She announced and walks into the kitchen. Looking around she grabs a knife from the drawer and walks back into the room as Ker'Shaun is trying to get dressed she announces. "And you. I ain't through. Before I leave this apartment; I'ma fuck you up." Jazz' Rae said while swinging the knife around. Ker'Shaun looks at Jazz' Rae and jumps over the bed with his pants dangling off of his ass; running down the hall. Jazz' Rae runs after him but Ker'Shaun manages to make it out the door. "You crazy man!" He hollered from the street. "You fragile fool! With your shit that you call a dick nigga please. My fingers can make me quiver and cum more then what you bring to the table." She hollered back. Walking back into the bedroom she grabs his belongings that been in her place ever since they started dating and throws it out unto the street. "Girl, what are you doing?" Ms. Annabelle shouted from the window with curlers rolled up tight to her scalp. "O nothing belle just some early spring cleaning and I do mean early." Jazz' Rae responded. Ms. Annabelle laughs "I see your man giving you troubles?" she asked. "Hell yeah, caught that lame cheating with another broad in my bed." Jazz' Rae said. Ms. Annabelle took a puff from her blunt "Alright now child go ahead and keep doing your thing and be good you hear me? Mama gotta go take a sip of that yak." Ms. Annabelle said. Jazz' Rae smiles "O I will." As Jazz' Rae finished throwing out Ker'Shauns belongings she walks into the bathroom to freshen up. "I then messed up my hair fooling with them mother fuckers. Shit!" looking in the mirror she notices her torn shirt "Look at my shirt. Dirty hoe then tore my favorite shirt." Jazz' Rae said. "I be damned." She mumbled.

Changing her shirt she pulls her curly hair back into a ponytail. She begins to clean up her bedroom and snatches the sheets from the bed that were now stained. Walking outside she throws the sheets next to the clothes in the street. The kids were playing on the block stopped to watch Jazz' Rae release her anger out on the materials that were now in the street. She rolls her eyes "What ya'll looking at?" she questions and walks

back into her place. "Dawg that's what type of chicks I like." The boy throws his hand down in excitement. "Those feisty ones can throw down when making up. Have yo boy satisfied for days." He said while smiling. Jazz' Rae walks over towards the sofa exhausted from work and fed up with relationships. All the hatred she held in filled her eyes and became tears. She couldn't believe what had just happened.

"O girl it will be alright." Nunu exclaimed. "There are plenty of fish in the sea, like my Grandma always told me; child don't you dare rely on a man to complete your happiness because if you do you ain't doing nothing but setting a trap for yourself." Nunu explained. Rubbing Jazz' Rae's back "And don't you cry over no sorry guy anyways. You too good for him to be mourning over something like that. He just lost out because first off he was staying at your crib he ain't pay no bills around here and he was eating your food. Broke fucker didn't have no money. That fool was jobless." Nunu said. Jazz'Rae laughed. "And what stupid broad want something like that. It doesn't take a rocket scientist to know that he wasn't worth nothing. I wouldn't have given him a time of my life. No offense." Nunu continued. Jazz' Rae looks at Nunu wiping her tears. " Man that was the last time I fall for something like that, but I still love him. As crazy as it sounds I do." Jazz' Rae said. "That's normal child don't sweat it." Nunu exclaimed wiping the tears from Jazz' Rae's face. "Yea you right." Jazz' Rae said. "Yeah I know. But girl I wish I could stay longer but my boss trying to get me to do some extra hours. And it doesn't hurt to make some extra money for side pleasure. Ya feel me?" Nunu exclaimed. "Yea." Jazz' Rae said. Standing up after their conversation Nunu holds out her arms and smiles Jazz' Rae walks up to her and gives her a hug. "Hang in there Ms. Thang." Nunu told Jazz' Rae before she left.

As Jazz' Rae flipped the channels on the T.V she started thinking. "How could I have not known he was cheating? He didn't have a job therefore he didn't have money to go no where but still came home late and he always smelled like sex and I know I kept soap, and I know damn well my water was running, matter of fact me and that fool haven't had sex in a hot minute." She continued to think amongst herself. "Phone calls from different broads every night. And I should have known when I met him at the club and he was surrounded with all them girls he was nothing but a player. Ugh I'm so stupid. Stupid, stupid, stupid. Jazz' Rae pouted and continued flipping the channels eating her favorite ice cream vanilla that was decked with sprinkles, pecans, and confetti cake. She called this particular dessert her masterpiece; at least that's what she thought of it. After scooping continuously she found herself at the bottom of the bowl no more ice cream meant no more happiness, settling under her blanket she moved into a fetal position and fell asleep.

Hearing a loud sound in her ear Jazz' Rae woke up to Nunu standing in front of her with two frying pans pounding them together. "Jazz' Rae get up! Girl I know not." Fiddling with her hair "Get up do something with your hair, take a shower, and eat we gonna go shopping. You single now boo. It's time to look it." Nunu exclaimed. Looking over to the clock it was only five in the morning. "No, no I'm going back to sleep." Jazz' Rae said. "No, no you getting your tail up so chop chop and get to the bathroom." Pulling on her arm Jazz' Rae finally got up and went into the bathroom. "Um Jazz why don't I hear water in there?" Nunu questioned. Jazz' Rae cuts on the water, sits on the toilet and bows her head wipes her eyes then pushed her hair back. She took in a deep sigh and started to undress putting one foot in after another feeling the shower mat under her feet she began to wash herself. Steam began rising up from the hot water falling unto her body. Seems as if she'd been in there for hours Nunu knocks on the bathroom door. "Hurry up girl." Nunu shouted. Jazz' Rae laughs "I'm coming I'm coming!" she said wiping the tears away that seemed to never stop.

As Jazz' Rae opens the door she and Nunu are face to face. Nunu standing with her arms folded. "Girl you've been in there for almost two hours, you know them malls on a Saturday be packed with people." Nunu said. "You act like my step-ma always rushing someone out of the bathroom." Jazz' Rae announced. She walks into the room and starts to get dress. Coming out and presenting herself in a neon sweater, white jeans with sandals that matched neither her shirt nor her pants. Nunu chuckles and then frowns. "O my goodness its eighty three degrees outside and you got on a sweater. If you don't get your narrow behind in there and change, matter of fact let me pick out your clothes." Nunu announced. Walking into the bedroom she opens the blinds to let the sun into the dark cold room. The warmness that hit the window and the sunlight that glared into the room was fulfilling. Nunu walks over to the closet and began to scramble through her belongings. "Nope, nope, definitely not. O yes!" Nunu announced. Pulling out a pair of black shorts and a red silky shirt that if a cool crisp of air were to hit her chess the girls would be welcoming people and saying Hi.

"Move it people we are trying to get through here!" Nunu shouted from the car. A little child around the age of three sticks his tongue at Nunu and then flicks her off. "You snotty little punk!" Nunu shouted and flicks the child off. "Nunu it's just a child." Jazz' Rae said. "Well that child acted like an adult so I'ma treat the lil punk like one." Nunu exclaimed. Nunu pulls in front of a car and slams on breaks, "Now what sucker I got this parking spot!" Nunu shouted while shaking her head at the other driver. "Nunu how many times I gotta tell you about your driving dang. You a dag on dare devil." Jazz' Rae said. Nunu held her lips together perking them up "So." Nunu exclaimed.

Walking through the mall a group of boys stood next to the Victoria- Secret store watching the women pick up panties and flaunt them in the air. Nunu shakes her heads "Guys act like they ain't seen panties before. This is a good example of immature." Nunu said. "I'm hungry." Jazz' Rae said. She walks over towards the bakery. "Um can I get a cup of coffee, with extra whip cream, and double the vanilla. And I want the donut with the raspberry filling please." Jazz' Rae said. Sitting down at the benches across from the shop, three other dudes are sitting next beside the water fountain looking at both Jazz' Rae and Nunu. One of the guys nods at Jazz' Rae; she smiles at him and he smiles back. His friend smiles at Nunu; and Nunu throws up her hand and shows her promise ring and smiles. The guy turns back around acting as if he didn't just hint at her; Nunu laughs. After Jazz' Rae finishes up with her quick bite she picks up her belongings and leave. Jazz' Rae and Nunu walk away hitting up every store that had a clearance sell. "I can wear this for my man tonight he hasn't gotten cutty from me since." She started counting on her fingers "since two days ago." Nunu said laughing amongst herself. "What you think Jazz, the pink see through or the silky black print?" Nunu questioned. "The pink see through." Jazz' Rae said. "Yeah you right." Nunu replied back. "Girl I remember when me and my man had sex mostly every night. I think he was a nymph on the real. After I started working those long hours we didn't have sex but so often. Damn and he knew how to make me weak." Jazz' Rae said. "Had me shaken and honey it was never cold." She said. "You still thinking bout that fool?" Nunu asked. "Yea he be jumping in my mind every second." Jazz' Rae exclaimed. Shaking her head Nunu announces "I'ma have to find you another man." "No I don't want another relationship right now." Jazz' Rae said. "Well at least let me get you a booty call." Nunu exclaimed. "Sex every night I don't see how you gonna live with out that." She said. "I don't want that either." Jazz' Rae responded. "Alright, alright." Nunu walks back into the dressing room pulls out her cell phone and began to dial numbers. "Hello, hey how you doing? That's good. Trying to sound all sophisticated on the phone boy. Yes you is don't be fronting but anyways I wanted to see if you could stop by my house. My man gonna be there just tell him you are there because I told you to come over. I think I got you something. Okay talk to you later" Nunu said. She walks back out the dressing room "Who was that on the phone?" Jazz' Rae questioned. "Nobody but my sister." "I bet it was. Girl you don't have no sister. You got three brothers fool. Who was that on the phone?" Jazz' Rae questioned again. Nunu tries to switch the subject "What you gonna do tonight?" Nunu questioned. Jazz' Rae looks at Nunu "Okay okay it was my brother's baby mama she wants me to baby-sit this evening. Dang all up in my business. But like I was asking you what are you doing tonight?" Nunu asked. "Mhm, I might go hit the club up tonight, haven't set it off in that bitch in a minute." Jazz' Rae said. "You know I would go with you but I get that daily dick." Nunu said. Laughing amongst herself "Nunu what I tell you about mentioning that in front of me?" She said. "Look it ain't my fault that you not getting any tonight if you would have kept that thing in check you would be taping it like me. Say no more." Nunu announced. "It ain't my fault either. If he want to be stuck with a bald headed scaly wag, with no ass then go right ahead. I was much too good for that low life anyways." Holding up her hands "Now see that's what I'm talking about. Bout time you see what I'm seeing." Nunu announced.

"Aye shawty what yo name is?" A male around the age of forty dressed in baggy jeans that showed his underwear and by meaning underwear he had leopard print with a small but noticeable stain on them. Around his neck was a gold chain from what was rocked in the eighties he slowly approached Jazz' Rae as he started speaking to her a mist of fragrance came from his mouth. Jazz' Rae squinched her nose up. "Man if you don't get your old busted ass up out of my face with your garlic breath, and that fake ass chain you wanna be Run DMC." She said. He grabs his glass with rhinestones glued onto them and walks away. "Old dirty bastard." She said. Then another guy approached her; he was on point in her mind. He was decked out from head to toe with his fresh clean hair cut, brown skinned, with a bad ass outfit but as he smiled she fell off of cloud nine. "Damn!" she said aloud. "Yo grill all jacked up!" she said, and walks away. He hollers out "How you gonna do me like that girl?" he questions. She turns around "Naw the question is how you gonna do me like that?" she opens up the door and walks out and he walks up to another girl.

"Shoot!" Jazz' Rae announced. "Late again are we now?" Her boss speaks aloud. "I over slept I had a real long night." She said. "A long night? I thought you and your dude broke up three weeks ago." Sheila announced. "Yeah we did but I went to the club Strawberries last night and let me tell you I will never go back there again. Ain't nothing but broke back mountain, retro, hillbillies up in there. The dudes are over twenty-six, they old fashioned, and they broke." She said. "I was just looking forward to having some fun but turned out to be a disaster." The bell above the door rang meaning there was another customer looking around the gentleman announces "I'm looking for a Jazz' Rae DaMarcus." He said. The workers and customers just stared at him. He was nicely dressed, well presented, built, with a tattoo on his neck that read thug till I die, but he was white. "Well!" Jazz' Rae announced. She stands up "That's me. I'm Jazz' Rae." He walks over towards her and puts out his hand. "What's up, I'm Quinton." She grabs his hand and starts shaking it. "Okay. What are you hear for?" she asks. "Your girl Nunu which is my homeboy's sister told me I could find you here." He said. " O really?" she questions. "Yea." "So yesterday evening was you the one that she told to come over her place?" Jazz' Rae asks. "Yea." I knew it, that punk then set me up Jazz' Rae thought to herself while starring at him then she smiled. I wonder if my hair is all right she thought to herself again while trying to fix it. "Well it looks like you are busy can we talk a little later?" He asked. "Yea sure hold on." She handed him a card "Give me your number and I'll call you." He had written his number on the card and left. Jazz' Rae rushed over to her cellular. "Nunu! I'ma get you girl." She said on the voicemail and hung up the phone.

"Rae don't be calling my phone talking about how you going to get me and you must have met my brothers friend. His name is Quinton." She said. "I know that already sending him to my job not giving me a head notice. What's wrong with you?" Jazz' Rae questioned. "You know I'm a match maker. I'm Nunu for goodness sakes." She announced. "Why Nunu? Why?" Jazz' Rae asked. "Because he is a cute looking fella and you my girl and I want some god babies." She said. "Huh. You know I don't do white bread." Jazz' Rae exclaimed. "O psh. That dude ok I know a good man when I see them. Trust me. Holler at the guy for a couple of days and see how it goes. I'm never wrong." Nunu said. "Okay you was the one that hooked me up with Ker'Shaun." Jazz' Rae said. "O girl it was just a fling I didn't think ya'll was going to go that far." Nunu announced. "I'ma give it a try but if it don't go well you paying me one hundred bucks." Jazz' Rae announced. "Alright girl I'ma get at you later." Nunu said. "Alright." Jazz' Rae responded back. "A hundred bucks my ass." Nunu said and hung up.

# Chapter Two-

## Off Brand

As she was just about to hang the phone up there was a surprising answer. “Hello!” Quinton hollered out. “Why is you hollering man? I can hear you.” Jazz’ Rae asked. “My bad, I’m just getting off from work.” “Where you work at?” “I work at a construction site. And I’m so use to hollering because of the loud noise that goes on around here.” Quinton announced. “O okay. It’s cool I thought you was hollering for no apparent reason.” “Na never that; so you decided to call me after all.” Quinton said. “Yeah I’m not the rude type.” She said in a sarcastic way. “You was looking at me like you didn’t even want to be bothered with me. Is it because I look white?” he asked. “What you mean is it because you look white? You are white from what I saw. And no.” she said. “Do you date white people?” he asked. “Na never have. That’s odd to me. Don’t ask me why it just is.” She said. “Why?” he asked. “Didn’t I just tell you not to ask me?” “Well I just want to know. Is it so hard to answer a simple question?” “Okay look I been around black people and Hispanics all my life and where I lived white people never liked a race different from them and the same went for me.” She said. “Well I love my black women, and I’m not just white I’m mixed with black too. I just got a real light complexion. No lie.” Quinton announced. Jazz’ Rae attitude changed quickly. “O really!” “Yeah shawty I bet you wanna talk to me now. That’s sad.” He said. “What’s sad?” she questions. “That you wanna talk to only your race. If I was just white I bet you would of hung the phone up a long time ago if I didn't tell you." He announced. "Stop putting me out to be racist I just grew up around that." She said. "And what's your race?" he asked. "I'm black mixed with Dominican, and my papa has Indian in him." She said. "Yea I can tell you got that sexy ass complexion on you with that long curly hair. Like to run my fingers through that" He said. "Ha, don't you wish. This hair is off limits sweetie." She announced. "O so it's like that I see." "It's like what?" she questions. "Can't let a brother go through the hair. What I got the cooties or something?" "Shut up! And yes you do have the cooties." The both of them laughed. "So I see you work at a barbershop. I know they don't have you cutting people's hair." He said. "Aha let me tell you something I can make you look like a million dollars. When I cut I get down to business ya dig? See I cut, braid, and after I'm done at the barbershop I go to the mall and work in the clothing store and on weekends I work at ladies foot locker. I gets good money, and I do good business. So you can hush honey." Laughing to himself "Girl I can tell already that you are a handful. Nunu told me that you a feisty one well I'ma tell you like this I like the feisty ones but like don't go to far because I only put up with so much." He announced. "Dude please. You can't handle this anyway." She said then hung up the phone.

"Nunu next time you try to hook me up with somebody me and you gonna have it out." Jazz' Rae announced. "What girl? What happened?" she said. "He told me that he not the type to take bullshit, and to let him know I don't take that either. So I hung up in his face straight up." She said. "Look here you need to calm your self down. You always getting all hyped up over something so small. Dang the dude was just telling you that he didn't take non-sense from nobody. So why you mad when you know you are the same way?" Nunu asked. "That's just how I am and you know this." Jazz' Rae announced. "Well you need to put yourself in check and stop acting like that." She announced. "Ugh whatever!" "Call him back and apologize for once. He didn't do nothing wrong." Nunu announced. "Okay!"

The fourth ring sounded off Jazz' Rae huffed in aggravation. "You have reached your boy Quinton I can't come to the phone leave a message and I might hit you up later one." Jazz' Rae took a deep breath in "Hey this Jazz' Rae if you don't mind can you hit me up later on?" she announced. She hung up the phone laid it on the sofa and walked to the bathroom. As she began closing the door the phone rang. "Hello?"

she questioned. "Hey!" he announced. "Hey!" she said back. "Umm are you gonna say something other then hey?" he asked. "Yeah my bad; Look I'm sorry for hanging up in your face and getting rude with you that's just how I am." She said. "Okay did you want to say you sorry or did somebody else tell you to apologize?" he questioned. "On the real though Nunu told me it was wrong and I do agree I just make small things out to be something big." She announced. "No hard feelings it's ight." He replied back. "So what are you up to?" he asked. "Umm I was going to the bathroom right before you called." She replied back. "O you need me to let you go?" "Na hold on for a second." She said "Ight." Jazz' Rae rushed back into the bathroom. "Okay I'm back." "Okay that was quick did you wash your hands?" he asked. "Yes I did." She replied back "Alright just making sure. So what you wanna talk about?" he questioned. "I don't know I'm use to the dudes starting up the conversation." She replied back. "Well we in trouble because I rely on the girls to start up a convo." He said. "Well how about we start from the basics? What's your first and last name and where are you from?" she questioned. "Ight my name is Quinton Allavero and I'm originally from Detroit. And you?" "Okay, okay my name is Jazz' Rae Nicole and I'm from Virginia." She announced. "What made you come to Atlanta?" he asked. "I came down here to stay with my grandmother because I stayed in trouble down in V.A and my ma got tired of me getting into trouble. Why did you come down to the A?" Jazz' Rae questioned. "Same with me but not because my mother sent me here I was caught up in some stuff and my girl got pregnant her parents didn't want me in the child's life because of my mistakes and they took her and fled. I was with my alcoholic dad and my work alcoholic mother and make a long story short I came down here to get away from the chaos plus my cousin hooked me up with this good paying job down at the construction site. Been here ever since." Jazz' Rae was interested in his story and wanted him to continue. "So you have a baby somewhere that you've never seen before?" she questions. "Yeah, Wild huh? I wish I could have been there I wanted a little solider of my own. I just can't believe her parents took her and moved without giving me any notice or anything." Quinton responded. "Wow. I was pregnant one time and I was a junior in high school. I was so struck up on the bad boys. You know? And he sold drugs, was involved in a gang, just wild and out there but I liked that. And I became pregnant just after about three months dating we were on and off throughout the whole thing. For one he couldn't keep his dick in his pants, and he was always running from the police. He got so drunk and just out of rage he slapped and shook me so hard then pushed me unto the floor and I had a miscarriage. He took the only thing I had left in life to live for. After that I just went down hill. So I was sent here." She announced. "Damn mama. I'm sorry about that." He replied. "It's okay I try not to think about it but every time I see somebody walking around pregnant or with their baby I just bow my head and look forward. And I'm sorry about the situation with your baby too." She said. "Thanks." He replied. "No problem." "So you feel comfortable talking to me a little bit?" he questioned. "Yeah. Just a little I don't really open up to people. Like the only person that knows me is Nunu she's like an angel to me she has been there for me ever since I came down here." She said. "I feel you little mama." He replied back. "You seem to be a cool chick. I want to chill with you sometime if you don't mind." Quinton announced. Jazz' Rae lit up with a warm glow and smiled. "Na I don't mind how about I come to your place sometimes. We all get together me; you, Nunu, and her boo. Sit and chill watch a movie." Jazz' Rae announced. "Aight no doubt how about Friday night. I'll be available then." "Available?" she asked. "Yeah available you know I work, and I got other stuff to do I'm a busy man." He said. Laughing amongst herself. "Yeah. Okay." She replied back.

Jazz' Rae walked up to the door beginning to knock but turns back and walks down the steps. "Lord! Is that you jazz?" CeeCee asked. Jazz' Rae turns back around and smiles "Hey grandma." "How you doing baby? Come on in." CeeCee said. Jazz' Rae squeezed through the opening and her grandmother. "Watch the toes now child. Can't afford you stepping on big mama's toes." She said. Jazz' Rae walked inside and sat on the couch. "Get up child don't come in here and not give your grandmother a hug." CeeCee announced. As Jazz' Rae stood up CeeCee announced. "You've then grown since the last time I saw you. Three long years, how you been child? What's going on since you got your apartment?" CeeCee questioned. "Grandma I been doing good, I not to long ago got out of a relationship. I found him cheating in my bedroom with some other skeet." She announced. "Jazz' Rae Nicole I told you that you shouldn't even mess with these young men right now. You have better things to do rather then spending your time with someone that doesn't even care about you." She said. Jazz' Rae nodded her head. "But see Grandma I thought he was a good person but I should have listened to you though. For some odd reason you are always right. Well when it comes to specific things." Jazz' Rae chuckled. CeeCee walked into the kitchen. "Have you talked to your mama lately?" She asked. "No maam last time I talked to her she was going out with her boyfriend for dinner." "O your mama go through more men then anything it doesn't make no sense." CeeCee said while coming out of the kitchen with some cookies. "Grandma what you make them for?" Jazz' Rae asked. "Me and my girls are going to have poker night." She replied back. "O okay." Jazz' Rae's phone began to ring "hello!" "Hey boo, did you call Quinton back?" Nunu questioned. "Yeah." Jazz' Rae turned to her grandmother and stood up. "Okay Grandma I'm going to get up on out of here. Don't bet all your money now." Jazz' Rae announced and hugged her. "I won't. Take care of yourself and don't wait another month to come see me either. I wanna see you in about two weeks from now." CeeCee announced and kissed Jazz' Rae on the cheek.

"Okay me and him were talking and we got along pretty well. He told me one Friday night to come over and invite ya'll too. I just don't know exactly what Friday. We gonna chill and watch a movie together." "Alright I'ma let Lamar know and we'll be over there." Nunu replied back. "Okay I'ma talk to you a little later on." Jazz' Rae announced. "Alright later." Nunu announced.

"Run girl run!" Nunu hollered out to the screen "Look see this is exactly what I'm always talking about. Why do the only black person in the movie get killed? Can't they survive for once?" Nunu said. They all began to laugh. "So when are you two going to hook up?" Nunu asked. Jazz' Rae looked up at Quinton from his lap as he looked down at her smiling at each other they didn't say a word. "O come on ya'll. You've known each other for six months now." Nunu exclaimed. "I know." Jazz' Rae replied back. "And?" Nunu questioned. "And you remember when I told you we were all going to chill and look at a movie together." "Yeah." "Well me and Quinton have been going out before that. And we just got in a relationship last week." Jazz' Rae announced. "Huh. Why am I the only one who didn't know? Lamar did you know?" Nunu asked. Lamar looked at her "Yeah." He said.

Nunu looked astound "Okay why am I the only one that don't know. You let this big head know before me." Nunu said. "What you mean big head?" Lamar questioned. "Baby you know I like your head. You be giving good brain." Nunu announced. "Too much information." Quinton hollered out. Nunu stuck her tongue at Quinton. "Okay we gotta get going. Congratulations to you two lovebirds. Though ya'll didn't tell me ahead of time." Nunu said. "Alright see ya'll." Quinton announced. Soon as the door closes Jazz' Rae speaks out. "What you up to tomorrow?" She questions. "Nothing chilling. Why what's up?" he asked. "I'm going to the mall and I want you to come with me." "Okay. But wait till about around three I get my check then." Quinton replied back. "Mhm. Okay." Locking lips Jazz' Rae exited out of the apartment and left.

# Chapter Three-

## We all Stumble

Looking into the window "O Q lets go up in here." Jazz' Rae announced. Picking up a shirt she holds it in front of Quinton's face. "You like?" she questioned. "Na. Who likes leopard print? Especially for a shirt. Come on now Jazz." He replied back. Jazz' Rae looks Q up and down. "Baby this would go cute with some skinny black jeans. I know what I'm doing here. You are looking at the fashion expert if I must say." She announced. Quinton smiled "Uh huh." As she continued looking through the large stock of shirts a guy appears in front of the two. Jazz' Rae looks up. "What are you doing?" she asked. "Nothing I'm just here with my girl Sharee." He replied back. Jazz' Rae looks over Ker'Shauns shoulder. "Is that her?" she questions. "Yeah." "Okay. But why are you over here?" she questions. "I been trying to call you." He said. "Yeah I know. I just didn't pick up the phone." Jazz' Rae announced. "Why?" Ker'Shaun questioned. "Because I don't want nothing to do with you." She said. "Okay." He looks over "Who is he?" he questions again. "This is my man. His name is Q short for Quinton." She announced. "O so you moving on I see." Ker'Shaun said. "Yea, what's it to you?" she questioned. "Ker'Shaun baby let's go." A voice from the other side of the department store interrupted the conversation. Ker' Shaun looks over "Ight. I gotta go. Deuces." He announced. Jazz' Rae throws her hand up twiddles her fingers rolls her eyes and turns back around. "I can't believe he came over here after the shit he did." She announced.

Quinton just stared at her. "Who was that?" he asked. "It's my ex boyfriend. Nobody important." She replied back.

"Nunu! Today up in the mall we ran into Ker' Shaun. And girl you won't believe this, but he got another girl." She said. "What he want? And what you mean believe, he is a decent looking dude he just too much." Nunu said. "Yea you right and he wanted to know why I haven't been returning his calls and text messages." Jazz' Rae announced. "That's good that you haven't been returning them though." Nunu announced. The doorbell rang "hold on I'm coming!" Jazz' Rae shouted. "Nunu I'ma get at you later." Jazz' Rae hung up the phone and attended to the knock. As she opened the door she stood in shock. "How dare you come back to my place after what you then put me through!" She announced. Ker'Shaun looked astound "Can I come in please?" he asked. Jazz' Rae lays her hand on the side of the door. "No!" she said. "Jazz just for a few minutes?" he asked again. "Please." He said. Jazz' Rae just stared at him. Shaking her head she knew she was about to make a mistake. "Alright come in." she said. Ker'Shaun entered into the apartment looking around he spoke out. "I see you changed the place up big time." He said. "Yeah I did some changes. New me with a new look." She replied back. Ker'Shaun just shook his head and sat down on the couch. Jazz' Rae walked over towards counter "So what you want?" she asked. "I'ma be straight forward with you. I want you back. I know you got a man and everything but I can't help but to think about you." He said. Not believing what he said Jazz' Rae questions. "So after cheating, not saying you sorry, and not seeing me for five months you all of a sudden want me back?" Ker'Shaun stands up walking towards Jazz' Rae. "I don't know what came on to me by cheating. I'm real sorry. Can you forgive me?" he questioned. "Yeah I'll forgive you but I won't forget about It." she said. "That's good enough for me." Grabbing a hold of her hands he questions again. "Do you still have love for me?" Jazz' Rae looks into his eyes and shakes her head "Yes. But not like I use to" She said. "Then why you with someone else?" Ker'Shaun questioned. "First off because I want to second he is a good person he knows how to treat me with some respect. And third he stays real with me even when it hurts." She announced. "I can prove to you that I'm a better person if you would let me. Just let me be with you. Come on baby we didn't have only bad times together. We had the good ones too, and even the better one's making love to you." He said. Jazz' Rae fell into the brief speech taking him by his head she kissed him on his lips. Ker'Shaun smiles and began kissing her again. Grabbing her thighs he lifts her as she wraps her legs around him. Pushing her up against the counter he slides her on top. He manages to take off her shirt, Jazz' Rae quickly stops him. And slides it back on. Just as she puts her shirt back down Quinton walks in, shocked to see what was going on he turns around and walks out. Jazz' Rae pushes Ker'Shaun out of the way and runs after Quinton. "Wait! Wait." She hollers out. Quinton starts up his car and speeds off. "Damn!" Jazz' Rae announced. Jazz' Rae walks back into her apartment and grabs Ker'Shaun's jacket and pushes him out the door. "What you doing?" he asked. "I'm showing you the way out." Jazz' Rae said. "Man whatever!" Ker'Shaun announced and threw up his hand. Jazz' Rae slammed the door behind her.

Running over towards the phone she starts to call Quinton. The phone just rang Jazz' Rae sighed then hung up. What did I get myself into? She thought to herself. Beginning to cry there was a knock at the door Jazz' Rae wiped away her tears and walked into the bedroom the knocking continued. Jazz' Rae finally gave in and answered the door. Opening the door Nunu was standing "O girl what's wrong with you?" she questioned. "Quinton caught me up in her with Ker'Shaun in the act." She announced. Shaking her head Nunu was quick to reply back. "I told you and I then told you. To stop letting Ker'Shaun back into your life he is a waste of your time nothing but drama comes from him." "I know." Jazz' Rae said. "No you don't know, because if you did you wouldn't of let him in your apartment in the first place. When will you learn that with every good thing there comes a consequence with it? You keep messing up you not gonna have nobody I know that's wrong to say but the truth got to be told sometime." Nunu announced. "I don't know you know I'm so use to it." Jazz' Rae said. "Well get your priorities straight, and fix it with Quinton." Nunu said. "Okay." She replied back.

# Chapter Four-

## Love Conquers All

"Two weeks!" Nunu shouted. "Two whole weeks, you haven't made any contact with Quinton. No phone calls, no physical contact. Dang what you waiting on?" Nunu questioned. "I don't know. Man I don't even know if I want to talk to the dude. He took this way out of proportion." Jazz' Rae announced. Nunu looked astound "Way out of proportion! What the hell is wrong with you? You stupid." Nunu hollered out. "Are you for real?" She questioned. "Yes. I'm tired of falling for these pitiful wimpy ass dudes that can't take stuff like a man." Jazz' Rae said. "You wilding shawty." Nunu said and left.

"Ugh" Jazz' Rae blew out in frustration. She grabbed her keys and left. Driving around the block she sighted Dre "Sup Dre?" she hollered out. "Nothing lil mama." "You up on there looking like a porch monkey." She announced. Throwing his hand up "Man shut up. Where you going?" he questioned. Jazz' Rae "I'm going down to Juicies house. Why you wanna go with me?" she asked. "Yeah. Hold on." He said. "So word around is that you and Shaun hooked up." He announced. "What? Who the fuck told you that?" she questioned. "I can't tell you all that." "Man don't fuck with me. Who told you that shit?" she questioned again in frustration. "Aight Shaun told me and the boys he said you weren't all that good. But he banged it like it was the last time he would get some cutty from you." He announced. "O hell naw. That low life didn't tap none of this I kicked his ass out my apartment. That wack ass fool with his two inch dick ain't nobody to me." She said. Laughing amongst hisself "Man that's too much information." Dre said. "Where your phone?" Jazz' Rae questioned. Dre hands her his phone "What you about to do?" he asked. "I'ma call his mama's house." She said. Dre began to laugh, "She don't like me any ways so it really doesn't matter." Jazz' Rae said. "Hello?" Ker'Shaun said. "You sho do have the nerve to go around telling people that you slept with me." "Girl it ain't nothing you know you wanted this from the get go." He said. "You never gonna change I swear. I feel sorry for the girl you with now. If she goes through the same thing I had to go through she in for a huge surprise. Glorifying a bastard like you ain't worth it. I'd never let you up in this pussy. I'd rather fuck your face and call it a day. You a scandalous fool grow the fuck up Ker'Shaun." Jazz' Rae said before hanging up. "Dang Ker'Shaun did some dirty stuff to you huh?" Dre asked. "Yeah he did. He is not the dude that he may seem to be. I had to learn the hard way. Now I've lost someone who treats me good." She said. Who? Dre asked. "This dude named Quinton Allavero." She replied back. "Quinton Allavero?" "Yeah." She said. "Light-skinned dude with blue eyes Quinton Allavero?" Dre asked again. "Yeah. How you know he light-skinned?" she asked. "Man that's my cousin." He said. "For real?" "Yeah. He took the looks after me." He said. "Ya'll were talking?" he asked. "We were together but he caught me with Ker'Shaun." She said. "Damn that's messed up shawty. And he didn't tell me nothing about this either." He said. "I know I feel sorry for it but I swear I didn't do nothing with Ker'Shaun we just kissed." "I'll see what I can do for you. He coming to my crib later on tonight, drop by around nine." Dre said. "Okay."

"Nunu I'm sorry for acting like a child. I know what I did was wrong but I'm frustrated." Jazz' Rae said. "I know you are girlie I've known you for awhile now and I know how you work. Just take things slow and stop rushing stuff." Nunu said. "Yes mama." Jazz' Rae said in humor. "That's right pudding." Nunu said. "What you doing?" Nunu asked. "I'm getting ready to go over Dre's place, I'ma go over there and talk it out with Quinton. I want him back, hopefully he want me back too." She said. "Well good luck mama, because once Quinton's mind is set he don't change it." Nunu announced. "Thanks." "No problem, later."

Jazz' Rae looks up at the house and then at her steering wheel. Walking into the room she see's Quinton, Quinton looks up meeting eye to eye with Jazz' Rae grabbing his belongings he daps Dre and Lamar and walks out. Jazz' Rae grabs Quinton. "Wait please." She said. The two walked outside feeling the crisp air once again Jazz' Rae rubbed her arms. "Quinton I just wanted to let you know that I am truly sorry. I didn't mean for that to happen. It was really my fault." She said. "I don't want to hear this." Quinton interrupted. "Please just hear me out." She said. Quinton huffed "Alright, what make it quick." He said. "Ker'Shaun came to my place and he was saying that he was sorry. And I had been with him for the longest time and I was in love with him. I guess it was just a phase. Once I got to know you I started thinking less of him. But what he said to me made me feel so much better like he actually felt wrong for what he did. You know. So I apologize for what I did." She said. Quinton smiled "It's all good little mama. I just wanted to hear a apology." Quinton said. Jazz' Rae smiled "Stop playing with me, but I'm sorry." She said. "Okay." He said. Jazz' Rae tugs Quinton on his arm and pulls him closer. "I love you." She said. "I love you too." He replied back. Dre and Lamar knock on the window starring at the two from the inside. "You a sucker for love." Dre hollered. Quinton looked up "Hater!" he hollered back. Jazz' Rae looked at Quinton "You a hater too." She said. "O there you go again." Jazz' Rae smiled up at Quinton.